THE
BRIDGE

KATHLEEN,

YOU ARE SUCH
A JOY AND BLESSING!
GOD BLESS
YOU
ALWAYS!

IN HIS GRACE,

THE
BRIDGE

LUISA WARD

Carpenter's Son Publishing

The Bridge

©2017 by Luisa Ward

Published by Carpenter's Son Publishing, Franklin, Tennessee

Published in association with Larry Carpenter of Christian Book Services, LLC of Franklin, Tennessee

Scripture taken from THE HOLY BIBLE, NEW INTERNATIONAL VERSION®, NIV® Copyright © 1973, 1978, 1984, 2011 by Biblica, Inc.™ Used by permission. All rights reserved worldwide

Edited by Christy Callahan

Cover and Interior Design by Suzanne Lawing

ISBN: 978-1-942587-95-8

Printed in the United States of America

DEDICATION

To my children Victoria and Cubie, III,
for believing in me since the day you were born.
I love you both with all my heart.

To my family and friends for your
unconditional love and support.

To Doug Inman, my college Sunday School Teacher who taught
me to live life to the fullest like he did. (RIP 9/07)
Thank you for the inspiration of this story.

To my mother Elizabeth, who gave me the passion to
write since I was young by reading her own work.
You are my favorite author.

To my earthly father Jesus, who always taught me to do
what I feared most, thank you because it led me to conquer
my fears and has taken me to where I am today.
Thank you Papi (RIP 11/15)

To my Lord and Savior Jesus Christ who has walked
by my side since I was 8 and shown me that ALL
things are possible with Him.

To the reader, may this story bless you, change you and
give you a passion to take time to make a difference in
others not as a movement but a way of life.

If you knew how you were going to die ...
would you change how you live?

CHAPTER 1

The pressure on Sarah's chest made it hard to breathe. Her face stung from the glass shards penetrating her skin, and her shoulder felt dislocated. Smoke burned her eyes and the stench of gasoline filled her nostrils.

Where am I?

Sarah could feel herself losing consciousness. Her chest tightened, and her breath came in short gasps.

What's happening?

Through the smoke she could barely make out the form of a man. The man, dressed in black, moved slowly toward her, one hand outstretched.

"Sarah, take my hand." he said in a calm, deep voice.

Who is this and how does he know my name?

Sarah bolted upright in bed. She was trembling and covered in cold sweat. Tears filled her eyes.

"Not again. Please, not again. God, why is this happening?" she whispered.

Sarah turned and lowered her feet to the cold floor. She stood still beside the bed for a full minute before plodding to the kitchen for a drink of water. She retrieved a glass from the cabinet, her mind filled with questions.

How many times have I had this same dream? How many days in a row? Who was the mysterious man dressed in black? And how do I know his name, Mordecai?

The dream disturbed her, and had happened with such frequency that she could vividly remember every detail.

Her world shrank after her twin daughters, Emma and Rose, were born. Steven, her now ex-husband, had walked out on her and their children. She had not forgiven herself for what had happened, and she certainly had not forgiven Steven. He had promised her the world when she was just sixteen years old, and then left her with nothing. She despised him for leaving, and though it meant her girls would grow up not knowing their father, she never wanted to see him again. Over time she became cynical, not trusting anyone.

Sarah did not dare tell anyone of the events of the last few months. Her life was pretty average and she did little to change that. She preferred isolation, and it seemed to have a grip on her. It was scary how good she had become at being alone.

Now, her days and nights were filled with uncertainty. The recurring dream had her rattled and her anxiety was crippling. The image of the man in black haunted her, and he knew her name.

What does this all mean?

She was overwhelmed with doubt, convincing herself she would go through the motions of life until fear had completely consumed her. Topping her list of fears was wondering what would happen to her daughters if something were to happen to her. The nightly visits from the man in black were beginning to affect her parenting skills.

Sarah questioned everything and everyone. She doubted the intentions of every person she met and was skeptical that any good people were left in the world. The thought made her sad, but she was good at hiding that side of herself.

I'm an Oscar winner, and I've never even been in a movie.

Those closest to Sarah would probably think she was having a nervous breakdown. She use to be so carefree and happy. She had lived in the moment and was spontaneous. But her cynicism, and the dream, had changed everything. It had changed her. It was also affecting her relationships with her coworkers, and customers, at Manhattan's Moon Rock Café. She had been rude with her coworkers and had even snapped at some of her regulars. Being a waitress for the last decade was wearing her down.

Her anxiety was growing more intense every day, and she questioned why she should care about anything. She desperately wanted to share her anguish with someone, but would anyone care? Would anyone believe the story of her nightly dream, or would they think she had lost her mind?

At the café later that day, Sarah stood in front of the mirror in the ladies' bathroom. She stared into her own eyes, looking for answers. All she saw reflecting back at her was emptiness.

Why is this happening to me?

She cut her break short and returned to work. Keeping busy was the only thing that brought her any kind of peace. She left the bathroom and returned to her place behind the counter. The sounds of the busy café helped to drown out the noise of her mind.

"God help me," she whispered to herself as she tied on her apron. She wondered when the last time was that she had uttered those words. It seemed like a lifetime ago.

The door to the café chimed and she looked up to see one of her regular customers, Mike Nelson, walking toward her. In addition to being one of her regular customers, Mike was a police officer and an old high school classmate. She put on her best fake smile, but Mike was not smiling. The expression on his face told Sarah that something was very wrong.

CHAPTER 2

Mike Nelson came to the café almost every day, and always around the same time. He would stay for more than an hour, and would chat with Sarah for most of that time. From the expression on his face, Sarah did not know if she was up for a visit this time.

Mike was tall and muscular, with salt-and-pepper hair and brown eyes. Those eyes had made her heart skip a beat for as long as she could remember, but he could never know that. Besides, being a cop was all Mike knew. He was forty-seven now, and had been a police officer since he turned twenty-nine. His father had been a cop, and Mike followed in his footsteps.

Sarah and Mike had remained close friends since their days in high school. They were there for each other during some very difficult times. Mike's father had been killed in the line of duty, and it was Sarah who Mike had leaned on for support during that time. After Sarah's husband walked out, Mike went to every Lamaze class, coaching Sarah until the day her daughters were born. They were close, and though neither of them talked about their friendship, each knew they could count on the other.

Sarah had grown used to their daily chats, which typically consisted of Mike's experiences as a cop on the streets of New York. It was all he talked about, and the stories were getting old. The daily reminder of the darker side of humanity served to underscore Sarah's skepticism about whether or not there were any good people left in the world. When Mike spoke of his experiences he became surly—proof they had their effect on him as well. Still, today Sarah would welcome the distraction his stories would provide.

Mike sat in his usual booth, which seemed to somehow be available every time he arrived. Reluctantly, Sarah walked over to the booth with a fresh pot of coffee. Mike liked his coffee black, strong, and extra hot. He glanced up at her expectantly, waiting for the question Sarah always used to open up the conversation.

"How are the streets today, Mike?" she said.

Mike watched in silence as Sarah tilted the pot, allowing the black liquid to spill into his mug. The rising steam carried the bitter scent to his nostrils.

"Okay, Mike, what's up?"

Mike let out a long sigh, still staring into his mug. "I'm not sure you really want to know."

"Of course I do. Hang on a sec, I'll be right back." Sarah stepped over to the counter and gestured to her fellow waitress, Liz.

Liz finished topping off a glass of water and walked over.

"Liz, I'm going to take a break." Sarah nodded toward the booth where Mike was seated. Liz smiled and Sarah hurried back to the booth and sat across the table from Mike.

"So, what is it Mike? You seem upset. Are the mean streets finally getting to you?"

Mike leaned over the table and looked right into Sarah's eyes. "I need to tell you something, but will you give me your word that it will stay between us?"

His intense stare, and unusual question, caught her off guard. They had shared many conversations over the years, but she had never seen him act this way. Even after sharing the most horrid stories from his job, he still managed to keep it together. Whatever was on his mind, it had shaken him to the core.

"Of course I do. What is going on, Mike?" Sarah's concern for her friend was growing.

"Honestly, I'm not sure if it's a good idea telling anyone, but if I don't get this outta my head, I'm gonna lose my mind."

Sarah was intrigued, and for the moment, had forgotten about her own troubles. "We've been friends since high school. You know as well as I do all of the secrets we've shared, so spill it."

Mike began talking, but Sarah's mind immediately drifted back to her own secret she had not shared with anyone. The haunting dream that had robbed her of sleep, and peace, for more days than she could remember. She tried to focus on what Mike was saying, but all she could hear was the deep voice of the man in black saying, *Sarah, take my hand.* A cold chill ran over her body.

Her mind was still drifting when Mike said something that snatched her from the shadows and dropped her back into the present moment.

"…dream every night, with the same man in black who—"

"Wait! What did you say?" Sarah's chill had turned into a cold sweat.

"Have you heard a word I've said, Sarah?"

"I'm sorry. I'm tired and my mind drifted for a minute. What did you just say about your dream?

"Look, this isn't easy for me so, I really need you to listen. If I don't talk about this with someone, I will go nuts."

"I'm sorry, Mike. I'm listening, really I am."

Mike took a drink of coffee and wiped his lips with the back of his hand. He took a deep breath, then started again.

CHAPTER 3

"It started a few weeks back. I woke up at 2 a.m. covered in sweat. I couldn't breathe. I just laid there with my heart pounding out of my chest. I had a dream I was dying, not gunned down like my dad, but in a multicar pileup on the Brooklyn Bridge."

Sarah could feel her heart racing. Each word that came out of Mike's mouth awakened within her the fear she had felt after her own dream.

"There I was," Mike continued, "people all around me crying and screaming. I think, in my dream, that I was coming back from the police station in Brooklyn, but I'm not sure. All I know is it happened so fast. I can't even tell you what caused the accident. I'm stuck in my squad car, trapped because my legs are pinned under the dash. Through the windshield, on the passenger side of my car, I can just make out the figure of a man walking toward me. He's dressed in all black. He walks up to the passenger door, leans through the broken window and says, 'Mike, open the door.' Then he starts tugging on the door handle. His voice was deep, but very calm. Almost peaceful."

Sarah was riveted to every word. He did not realize it, but Mike was describing her dream almost verbatim. Her mind tried in vain to convince her it was impossible for them to have had the same dream. Yet here it was, facing her head on. Right down to the mysterious man in black with the deep voice. She had a dozen questions she wanted to ask, but she did not dare interrupt.

Mike was a seasoned police officer with years of experience on some of the toughest streets in the nation. He did not rattle easily, and he kept his composure in tense situations, but he was visibly shaken.

Mike continued, "I started to feel cold, I knew my legs were trapped and I knew I was losing blood. But there was nothing I could do. Somehow, I knew I had only minutes to live. All around me people were screaming for help, but I could not help them. Even now, I can see their faces, pleading for me to help. I kept shouting at the man to go help them, but he ignored my cries. He just kept tugging at the door handle and asking me to open the door. Over and over."

Another sip of coffee, another deep breath. "My radio wasn't working and my cell phone had been thrown into the floorboard, out of reach. I had no way to call for assistance. I felt helpless. I haven't felt that way since dad was killed. The worst part is that I keep having this dream. Every single night for weeks, and it is the exact same dream. Same scene, bridge, people, and the same man in black.

"I apologize for my language, but I am just so tired of this shit! I feel like I am literally losing my mind. I mean, what I am supposed to do? How do I make these dreams stop? You know what bothers me the most? How in the hell does that man in black know my name? None of this makes any sense. Maybe I've already lost it. What makes this even more bizarre is that I know his name Sarah. His name is Mordecai!"

Sarah was stunned. She could not believe what she had just heard. How was it possible for her and Mike to have been having the same dream, and not just once but dozens of times?

Mike must have noticed the fearful expression on Sarah's face. "What is it, Sarah? What's wrong? You've heard me tell hundreds of terrible stories and I have never seen that expression on your face before. You think I'm nuts, don't you?"

"No, I don't think you're nuts, Mike. Or … if you are, then so am I."

Mike drew back, as if confused. "What are you talking about?"

"Your dream. I have been having the same dream for weeks. Only in my dream, the man in black is telling me to take his hand."

"What?" Mike raised his voice "That's not possible. Are you trying to make fun of me? I thought if I could share this with anyone, it would be you. How can you joke about this?"

"I'm not joking. I am dead serious, so enough with the accusations."

Mike stood up, then looked down at Sarah. "You know, not everything is about you, Sarah. I thought you could help me understand this craziness, but never mind. Thanks for the coffee and just put it on my account."

"Mike! Please let me explain," Sarah pleaded.

But he was already walking away.

She sat motionless in the booth, in a state of shock and disbelief. The past few minutes with Mike felt as surreal as the dream that apparently haunted them both. She heard the chime of the door and knew he was gone.

CHAPTER 4

Sarah didn't know how long she stayed in the booth after Mike walked out, but it felt like hours. Her head was spinning with disbelief.

Finally, Liz walked over to the booth and snapped her back to reality. "Sarah? Are you alright?"

"Huh? Oh, yes. I'm fine, Liz."

"Well, do you mind helping us out? We have several tables waiting and orders are starting to pile up."

Sarah scooted out of the booth and walked back to the counter. She would finish the shift, but she had to get in touch with Mike. She had a sinking feeling he would not be back the next day, and she didn't want to wait that long anyway. She fought the urge to call him, but she knew he needed some time to calm down before hearing from her. He was a proud man and it had not been easy for him to share about the dream. He had misunderstood her reaction and it had bruised his ego. No, she would wait till her shift was over and then give him a call.

How many nights would she have to endure that dream? She desperately needed to talk to someone about it, and now it was clear that person was Mike. Maybe the two of them could figure out why the dreams had started in the first place, or more importantly, how to make them stop.

It was plain to Sarah that Mike was having just as much trouble dealing with the dreams as she was. She had not seen him that upset since his father was killed, and that had happened years ago. The fact was that most things did not get to Mike. He had a kind of emotional shield that protected him from all but the most serious situations. The recurring dream had shaken him, and that was no small matter.

Sarah knew that if anyone could understand what she was going through it was Mike. Would he give her a chance to explain? If he would just hear her out, see how the details of her dream were nearly identical to his, he would believe her. The only differences in their dreams were that she was in a city bus, while Mike was trapped in his police car, and that this man in black had spoken to them, and they both possibly knew his name. Everything else was the same.

She glanced at the clock on the wall. Two more hours until her shift was over, and then she would call Mike.

*****

Mike paced back and forth inside the locker room of his precinct. He was angry that Sarah tried to spin their discussion into something about her. How could she do that? It wasn't the first time she had done it, but this time it really got to him. It had not been easy going to the diner and spilling his guts. He had hoped that talking with Sarah would help him figure things out, but that plan went south, along with his mood.

In high school, it had always been Sarah who came up with the best story to explain to teachers why they were late for class. They always believed her too. He thought it was cool at the time, but not so much when she tried to use her storytelling skills on him. Why would she do that? There was just no way she was having the same dream. She was just seeking attention.

The trouble was, he didn't have anyone else he could confide in.

CHAPTER 5

Beth worked hard trying to organize her desk. The clutter was stressing her out, and she had to do something about it. She paused for a moment to assess her progress. So far, so good.

If I could only declutter my mind as easily as my desk.

Beth was an attorney at the law offices of Jones, Buchanan & Williams. She was five feet three with dark brown hair, and even darker eyes. Her pale complexion betrayed the fact that she spent most of her time indoors. She began her career as a legal aid to Mr. Jones seven years ago. He had been the partner, and law school roommate, of her uncle Henry. She worked her way through law school and joined the firm after graduating. She loved her job and took it seriously, but the last three weeks had been especially hard.

Born Catherine Elizabeth Sanchez, and one of nine children, Beth had been exposed to the world of law at an early age. She was from Canastota, a small farming community in upstate New York. Her favorite uncle, Henry, had been a prominent attorney in town. Throughout her high school years, Beth would visit her uncle's law offices nearly every day after school and watch him work. She learned a lot from him and decided to follow in his footsteps and attend law school.

Uncle Henry later moved to Brooklyn and joined the firm where Beth now worked. After graduating she followed her uncle to Brooklyn and got hired on at the firm as Mr. Jones' legal aide. She worked hard and quickly developed a reputation as a fierce lawyer.

But something inside of her changed when Uncle Henry died. She grew cold and distant. Somewhere along the way, she had lost her idealistic views and began focusing on winning, no matter the cost. And win she did.

She won at least twice the number of cases as other lawyers in the firm.

Beth had paid a price for her ambition. Her social life was nonexistent and the years behind her were littered with broken relationships. The job had become her life and her only refuge. She was far from the person she had dreamt of becoming, but with each year that passed she cared a little less.

Beth picked up a stack of pending case files and arranged them into a neat pile. She placed them on the corner of her desk and sat down in her chair. Her desk was now clear and organized, her mind not so much. The dream was taking a toll on her.

Why is this happening? What does it mean?

She swiveled around in her chair and put her elbows on the desk. Holding her head in her hands, she made the decision to leave the office and go to one of her favorite coffee shops. She needed to think, and try to figure out the dream that tormented her every night.

Beth stood up, grabbed her purse, and walked to the door. She paused, looked back at her desk and the pile of files. They would have to wait. She turned off the lights and closed the door.

CHAPTER 6

New York City traffic, and the cacophony of car horns that came with it, were making it difficult for Frank to think. His knuckles were white as he gripped the steering wheel, and his patience was wearing thin.

I'm getting too old for this.

Frank had been driving a cab for twenty-two years. He had worked a few odd jobs when he was younger, but looking at life through the windshield of his cab was all he knew. He had never married and lived alone, and did not socialize with anyone outside of work. His home in Briarwood, a small community in Queens, was simple and sparsely furnished. His only hobby, if one could call it that, was doing repairs on his cab. His life was simple, and that was how he liked it. However, the past few weeks had been anything but simple.

The dreams began almost three weeks earlier. Every night it was the same thing. He was involved in a multicar pileup on the Brooklyn Bridge. He was trapped inside of his cab, hearing the cries for help from other motorists. Then, out of the chaos, a man dressed in black approached his cab and called him by name.

Frank was disturbed by the dream for a number of reasons. One was the fact that he never went to Brooklyn, and therefore would have no reason to be on the bridge. Another thing was that he never had dreams, or if he did he never remembered them. Now, he was not only having the same dream every night, he remembered every single detail.

Why is this happening? Who is the mysterious stranger who knows my name? And how do I know his his?

He had so many questions but no answers.

The fact that the dream took place on the Brooklyn Bridge was puzzling. In all of his twenty-two years of driving a cab, Frank never had a fare in Brooklyn. It was not a part of the city that he serviced. It did not make any sense.

Then, two days later, something happened that sent chills down his spine. His boss, Joe, asked him to go to Brooklyn to pick up a customer. Frank questioned Joe about the fare and asked if another driver could go instead. Joe had insisted that Frank be the one to go, and asked him to radio back when he had picked up the customer. He told Frank that he would be going into Brooklyn to pick up this client every Tuesday afternoon for the next month.

He could not get any more details from Joe, and did not want to push his luck by inquiring further. He needed the job.

Frank felt like he was living out an episode of the Twilight Zone. In twenty-two years of cab driving, he had never gone to Brooklyn. Now, these dreams plagued his nights, and his boss asks him to go to the very place of his nightmares. He did not want to do it, but he couldn't simply refuse to go without a legitimate reason. He couldn't tell his boss about the dreams. Not a chance. He would think Frank was nuts and probably fire him, and that frightened him more than going to Brooklyn. Being a cab driver was all he knew, and he was too old to start something new

Why me? Am I losing my mind?

His mind wandered back to the dream. Trapped in his cab,

the man in black calling his name, and the cries for help.

Frank's fingers gripped the steering wheel, and a chill crawled up his spine.

CHAPTER 7

The man in black and the cries for help were not the only things Frank remembered about the dream. He could clearly remember that the fare in Brooklyn was a female lawyer, and that she was trapped in the back of his cab. He could not see her face, but her cries for help were seared upon his mind. He could not help her because he, too, was pinned.

I just want it to stop. Please.

The first day Frank made the trip to Brooklyn, per Joe's instructions, things got really weird. When he arrived at the address he discovered it was a law firm, and the client he picked up was a woman. The woman was a lawyer.

Could this be her? Is this really happening?

After his second trip to Brooklyn, and the long ride back across the bridge to Manhattan, he had several conversations with the woman. The more he talked to her, the more he was convinced she was the woman from his dream. Even her voice was the same.

How is this possible? Is it a premonition of what's to come?

Frank desperately wanted answers, but who could he ask? There was no one he could talk to who would not think he was crazy.

Frank went to bed late that night, dreading what he knew would happen. Finally, he fell into a fitful sleep, only to find himself back on the Brooklyn Bridge, trapped, his cab filled with stifling fumes, and the cries for help coming from the back seat. He watched as the man in black approached the cab.

Mordecai.

The name was thrust into his thoughts. Instantly, he knew it was the name of the unknown man.

Mordecai walked to the driver's door, leaned down, and peered through the shattered window at Frank.

"Frank, open the door." Mordecai said, tugging on the door handle.

Frank woke up, startled. He stared wide-eyed into the darkness, his heart pounding in his chest. Once again he was covered in sweat, and each breath was a struggle.

He sat up on the edge of the bed, then switched on the lamp on his bedside table. He opened the drawer and retrieved a notepad and pencil. Ever since the dreams had started, he had kept track of how often they happened. This was night number twenty-one.

He set the pencil down and stood up from his bed. He peeled off his sweat-soaked shirt and stumbled his way to the bathroom. He squinted his eyes when he flipped on the lights. He bent over the sink and splashed cold water on his face. He straightened up, looked at himself in the mirror. Dark circles under his eyes were evidence of how much sleep had eluded him over the past few weeks.

Who is Mordecai? Is he real?

Frank wondered if the dreams were some kind of message. But if they were, what kind of message and from whom?

He knew that if he didn't figure it out, the dreams would never stop.

CHAPTER 8

George was busy placing barricades around the new construction site on West 57th Street, just a block away from Moon Rock Café. The building renovation would soon begin and it was necessary to divert sidewalk and street traffic accordingly. George enjoyed physical labor, which is why he had been attracted to a career in construction and demolition in the first place. He was about five feet eight and fit. He lived alone, had no close friends, and his job was his life. His average work day was sixteen to eighteen hours long, and he did not tire easily. However, the thoughts racing non stop through his mind was wearing him down.

It started almost three weeks earlier. It had been an ordinary day. Sixteen hours on the job, a quick dinner he prepared himself, and then bedtime. That is when things went from ordinary to unusual. Like many people, George occasionally had dreams. He seldom remembered much about them, and they were typically related to his work. That night was different.

Not one night had passed, since that first night three weeks ago, where he did not have the exact same dream. He was on the Brooklyn Bridge, there had been a serious accident, and many voices crying out for help. In the dream, George was on the ledge of the bridge, with the East River streaming by far below. Out of the din of screams and smoldering metal came a mysterious man dressed in all black. Somehow, George knew the man's name was Mordecai, and even more disturbing was that Mordecai knew George's name. He would walk toward George with his outstretched hand, calling his name.

Now, sleep was a distant memory and George did not know how much longer he could hold up. The long days, and even longer nights, were taking a toll on him.

He was startled out of his reverie by the blast of a car horn. He had been so distracted by his thoughts about the dream that he had begun placing barricades on undesignated streets.

God, I am losing it.

For the first time in his life, George was afraid of the night. He knew that with the setting of the sun, the dream would rise again into his consciousness and steal away any chance of rest.

Who is Mordecai? What does he want with me?

A little more than two years ago, during a huge restoration project, George had spent a lot of time on the Brooklyn Bridge. He had not been back since, but now the bridge came to him in his dreams. It made no sense, and he didn't know if it could take it much longer.

CHAPTER 9

Sarah glanced over at Mike's favorite booth. It had been several days since she last saw him, and their last visit had not ended well. She tried calling him, three times in fact, but he never answered. She would never tell him so, but she missed seeing him.

She wanted the chance to explain, to let him know that she understood what he was feeling. If he would give her an opportunity to share the details of her own dream, he would see she was telling the truth. The dream that plagued his nights also plagued her own.

Maybe there's a reason we're both having the same dream.

Sarah considered going to the precinct where Mike worked, then quickly dismissed the thought. She would not disturb him there or make him feel uncomfortable around his fellow police officers. She resolved to wait it out and hoped he would return to the diner soon.

Sarah wondered why Mike would think she would lie about the dream. She would never do something to intentionally hurt him.

He'll come around.

The sound of the café door chime drew her attention away from the empty booth. It was Mike.

Mike looked at Sarah, smiled sheepishly, and walked over to the booth. He sat down just as she arrived with a pot of fresh coffee and a mug.

"Hi, Mike. Coffee?"

"Yes, please. Do you have a minute to talk?"

"Sure. I'm going to return this coffee pot and I'll be right back. Okay?"

Mike nodded and Sarah scurried back to the counter. She sat the pot down and slid it across the counter to Liz.

She leaned over the counter and whispered, "Liz, I won't be long. I promise."

"No worries, the tables are covered. Take your time."

Sarah slid into the booth across from Mike. She was nervous and could feel her heart racing. She braced herself for what was coming.

Mike stared into his coffee cup, trying to summon the courage to speak. "Sarah, I owe you an apology."

"What? An apology for what?" Sarah was stunned. She had expected Mike to still be angry.

Mike finally looked up from his coffee. "For the way I talked to you the last time I was here. I was upset and I took it out on you."

"It's okay, Mike, really."

"No, it's not okay. We've been through alot together over the years, and I should have known you'd never lie to me. Especially about something like this."

"So, you believe me?"

"Of course I do, but I'd be lying if I said that it made me feel any better. If anything, it freaks me out. How is it possible that we're having the same dream, and what the hell does that mean?"

"I have no idea," Sarah admitted. "But it freaks me out too."

"I didn't let you finish your story last time. Tell me your

version of the dream."

Sarah's eyes filled with tears. She was grateful that Mike believed her, and even more grateful that she had someone she could talk to about the dream. "Okay." She leaned back and took a deep breath. "It started a little more than three weeks ago. The first night it happened, I didn't think much of it. I figured it was just a nightmare, you know. But then it happened again ... and every night since." Sarah leaned forward and folded her hands on the table. "I just want them to stop."

Mike patted her hands. "I know. So do I, but maybe talking about this will help."

Sarah nodded. "I'm in the middle of a huge pileup, just like you described from your dream. I am on a city bus, returning from somewhere. I'm not sure where I had been. I'm trapped on the bus, there's glass in my face, and I can hardly breathe. I can hear people crying out for help, all around me, but I cannot move. Then a strange man, dressed in black, walks toward me, reaching out his hand and calling my name. He asks me to take his hand. In the dream, he never says his name, but I somehow know it."

"Mordecai." Mike spoke in a low whisper.

Sarah felt an icy chill run down her spine. "Yes. It's weird, but in the dream I'm not afraid of him. He doesn't appear to be injured, his clothes are spotless, and he seems strangely calm considering what's going on around him. What does it mean? Is Mordecai supposed to be the angel of death or something?"

CHAPTER 10

Mike sat motionless, once again staring into his coffee mug. He did not have the answers to Sarah's questions, but he felt sure of one thing. None of this was a coincidence.

He cleared his throat and drank the last of his coffee. "I can't explain any of this or why it is happening. I feel sure that it's not a coincidence that we are both experiencing the same dream every night. The important thing to remember is that we are not going crazy. All of this means something and we'll figure it out. One way or another."

"So what are we gonna do, Mike?"

Mike slid out of the booth and stood looking down at Sarah. "I don't know yet, but let's talk again tomorrow. We will figure this out together, just like we have with everything else we've faced over the years." He took Sarah's hand, helped her out of the booth and gave her a quick hug. "I'll see you tomorrow, okay?"

Sarah nodded and watched Mike as he weaved his way through the tables and out the door. She felt more peace at that moment than she had in many weeks. They had not solved the riddle of the dream, but they were no longer facing things alone. It had been too long since Sarah had felt hope, and the feeling brought a smile to her lips.

Thank you, God.

Her shift was almost over and all she could think of were her children, Rose and Emma. Soon, they would have their mom back. Her kids were smart, and knew something had been going on with their mom. They were only eleven years old, but they knew.

When Sarah got home from work, Tori, her sitter, informed her that the girls had finished their homework. They had also taken their baths and were in bed, reading and waiting for their mom to get home to tuck them in. Sarah thanked her and walked her to the door.

"See you tomorrow," Tori said. "Good night and sleep well." Sleep well.

Sarah repeated those words in her mind. She could not remember the last time she had slept well.

She tucked her girls in bed and kissed them good night. "I love you. Sweet dreams." She flipped off the light. She wished her own dreams would be sweet.

Sarah got herself ready for bed, and when she finally crawled under the covers, she was afraid to close her eyes. She knew what awaited her in her sleep.

God help me. Here I go again.

Sarah wondered if God even cared. She had turned from her belief when her husband left. That seemed like a lifetime ago.

Maybe God does care. Maybe he sent Mike to help.

Somehow, she would get past all of this. She had to, for the sake of her daughters. She could not bear the thought of what would happen to them if something happened to her. She hoped that this would soon be over. It had to be.

CHAPTER 11

Sarah couldn't move. The bus was on its side, twisted and mangled from the collision. The smoke and fumes made it nearly impossible to breathe. She gasped for air as she watched a shadowy figure approach the bus. The dark figure grabbed her by the hand and pulled her from the wreckage.

Sarah awoke with a start. Once again, she was covered in sweat and her heart was pounding. She lay there, her chest rising and falling as she tried to normalize her breathing. She could still smell the fumes and hear the cries. It was as if the dream refused to release her from its grasp, even though she was awake.

Why is this happening to me? What have I done to deserve this?

Or was it something she hadn't done. That thought stuck in her mind and she sat up in bed. "God, is that it? Is there something I haven't done?" she asked, staring up at the ceiling. It had been a long time since she had prayed in any form or fashion. Her mother had taught her how to pray when she was just a child, but prayers and hope left with her husband it seemed.

Still, the short prayer she had just uttered brought her peace and she felt calm. Those feelings compelled her to pray aloud again. "God, it's been a while, I know. Please help get through this and help me find answers. Amen."

It felt good talking to someone bigger than herself. The feelings of peace and calmness stayed with her, and she drifted off to sleep.

CHAPTER 12

Sarah could not wait to get to work. She was anxious to start the day. And to talk to Mike. She had to share with him about the dream, and how it still seemed real after she woke up. She also wanted to tell him how she had felt after she prayed.

She hurried down the sidewalk and was about to enter the café when she heard Mike's voice. She glanced quickly around and spotted him down the street standing between two men. One man was a construction worker, complete with yellow vest and hard hat, the other a cab driver. The two men appeared to be having an argument, and Mike was playing referee.

Sarah walked down the sidewalk and right up to where the men were standing. "What's going on?" she asked.

Mike was obviously surprised to see Sarah on the street. "Sarah, just go to the café. I'll be there in a few minutes."

"Mike, we need to talk." Sarah stood her ground. She had no intention of leaving.

"Okay, Sarah, just give me a minute. Let me straighten things out between these two."

After what she had experienced last night, Sarah was not about to walk away. She had no idea what these men were arguing about, but it couldn't be more important. She stepped over and placed her small frame squarely between the two men. "Now, you two listen to me. I don't know what you're arguing about and I don't care. You have two choices. You can continue this nonsense down at the police station, or you can come sit down in the café and talk it out like grown men." She pointed emphatically toward Moon Rock Café as she spoke.

The two men stared at her wide-eyed. They each glanced at Mike, who was also staring wide-eyed, and then back at Sarah. Obviously outmatched, all three men lowered their heads and shuffled off toward the café.

*****

Mike allowed the two men to enter the café first, then paused outside the door with Sarah. "What has gotten into you? I have never seen you so full of fire and sass."

Sarah leaned in close to Mike. "After what happened in my dream last night, I had to talk to you. I woke up and still smelled the fumes and heard the people crying for help. It was like it was still happening, but I was definitely awake. Then, the mysterious Mordecai pulled me from the bus."

Mike looked stunned, though he shouldn't have been. He had a similar experience in his dream last night and had awakened with the smell of fumes and smoke still present.

Moon Rock Cafe was just opening, so there were still several tables to choose from. Sarah led the cab driver and construction worker to a booth, and Mike went to his usual spot a couple of booths away.

After Sarah had the men seated, she motioned to Mike with her finger. He obeyed and walked over and stood beside her.

Sarah turned her stern gaze toward the men sitting down. "You two make this fast. Officer Mike doesn't have all day to play referee, and besides, I need to talk with him. Are we clear?"

The men looked at her sheepishly and nodded in agreement.

"Good. Get started, and I'll bring you some coffee. On the house."

Mike shook his head as he watched Sarah walk away. He pulled up a chair and sat at the head of the table. "Okay, gentleman, I suggest we make this quick or we'll have to deal with her."

Both men smiled uncomfortably and nodded.

Mike discovered that the cab driver's name was Frank, and the construction worker was George. Apparently, what had sparked the argument was the fact that George had inadvertently placed a barricade on the wrong street, directly in front of Frank's cab. George admitted his mistake and apologized to Frank. Frank apologized for overreacting and the two men shook hands.

"Well, that was easy enough," Mike said. "Why don't you two sit here awhile and enjoy your coffee. I'll be right back."

Mike walked back to his booth and sat down.

As if on cue, Sarah arrived with a cup of coffee. "I only have a few minutes. We'll be getting busy soon and Liz will need my help."

Mike agreed. "Let's cut to the chase. I experienced pretty much the same thing you did. I woke up and it felt like the dream was still going on. I could hear and smell everything, just as if I was actually there."

"Yeah, me too. That's exactly what it seemed like to me. Something else that was new was that man pulling me out of the wreckage. He kept saying my name, it was as if he knew me. He actually said, 'It's me, Mordecai. Take my hand.' It all seemed so real, and when I woke up it felt like it was all still happening."

Sarah noticed that while she was talking, the construction worker kept glancing at her, like he was trying to listen in on her and Mike's conversation. She lowered her voice and continued. "What are we going to do, Mike?"

Mike glanced over at George and Frank.

They seemed to be fine and were quietly talking.

"Sarah, in the dream, do you have any idea why you are on the bus? Where you are coming from or where you're going? Are you alone?"

Sarah shook her head. "No. All I know is I'm on the Brooklyn Bridge. I have no idea why." She paused. "What are we going to do? How do we make this stop? I don't know what would become of my girls if something were to happen to me. Are we destined to die on that bridge? Is that what this is all about?"

Mike leaned across the booth and took Sarah's hand. "This is not our destiny. I may not know what all of this means, but I refuse to believe that any of this points to our deaths. We just have to figure out what it does mean. Okay?"

"Okay," Sarah said, brushing away tears.

They sat in silence for a few minutes, each lost in their own thoughts. Then the sound of the door chime interrupted their silence. Three customers walked in and sat at a table.

Sarah squeezed Mike's hand and stood up. "I need to help Liz with these customers. I shouldn't be long. Can you stay?"

Mike nodded and Sarah hurried away.

She didn't want Mike to leave until she had the chance to tell him about what happened after the dream last night.

CHAPTER 13

Mike waited as Sarah rushed around taking care of her customers. He walked over to where Frank and George were still seated and wished them a good day. He had just made it back to his booth when Sarah returned.

"Mike, thanks for hanging out. I wanted to tell you more about last night. Specifically, what I was thinking after waking up from the dream. I was asking why this keeps happening. I wondered what I had done to deserve this. And then it hit me."

Mike's had a puzzled expression on his face. "What do you mean?"

"What I mean is that when I asked myself what I had done to deserve this, a different thought popped into my head. Maybe it is something I have not done. Maybe that's the key."

"I'm not sure I follow."

"Have you ever thought about what you do for others? I don't mean anything about your job either. Can you think of anything that you do for others on a regular basis that is all about them, and not for yourself? Think about it. I did, and I wasn't so pleased with my answer. We are both so caught up in our own lives that we aren't thinking of others. We both have things in our past that we have not let go of, and those things drag us down. It has changed us, and not for the better. We have held on to all of the crap life has thrown at us, and for what? We've become cynical and bitter. Maybe this dream is trying to tell us to change, before it's too late. Maybe letting go is the bridge that will take us away from these maddening dreams and to a more peaceful life. Maybe we need to forgive others … and ourselves."

Mike cleared his throat before he spoke. "I've never heard you talk like this before. Where is this coming from?"

"I'll tell you, but you have to promise me you won't laugh." Sarah smiled.

"Okay, I promise I won't laugh."

"After the dream woke me up last night, and I started having those thoughts, I prayed."

"That's it? You just said a prayer and everything was okay?"

"That was the first time I'd prayed in years. I guess I'd stopped believing in such things, especially after Steven walked out on me and the girls. This dream has turned my life upside down Mike, and after I prayed last night I was at peace. It got me thinking outside of myself, something I have not done for a very long time. Maybe that's the point of all of this. Maybe we need to start thinking and caring for others, and perhaps that's where we start and where the nightmares end."

CHAPTER 14

George and Frank were getting along nicely. They each shared a little about their background and how they came to do what they did for a living.

George was still a little distracted by the bits and pieces of the conversation between the cop and the fiery little waitress. He was sure he had heard the waitress mention a man in black and something about a dream. He had almost convinced himself he was mistaken when he clearly heard the word *bridge*. It was as if they knew about his dreams.

That isn't possible.

George was tempted to walk over and ask them what they were talking about. He was desperate to talk to someone—anyone—about what he had been experiencing.

*****

Frank could tell that George was only half-listening to him talk. He wasn't doing much better himself. His attention was being drawn to the waitress and police officer. He wasn't entirely certain, but he thought heard them talking about the Brooklyn bridge and a man in black. His thoughts drifted to his own dreams, and the notepad by his bed which revealed how many times he had awakened in the night in a cold sweat.

"Well, I better get back to work," George said, interrupting Frank's thoughts. "Nice meeting you, Frank."

"Yeah, same here. Sorry about the misunderstanding."

They slid out of the booth, shook hands, and headed for the door.

*****

George passed by the booth where Mike and Sarah were talking. He almost stopped and asked them about their conversation, but fear triumphed and he walked on by. He merely nodded at Mike and kept moving.

As George walked out he thought, *At least I know where I can find these two if I dare talk to either one about these dreams.*

*****

Frank walked over to the booth and thanked Mike for his intervention.

"You are welcome, Frank. You caught me on a good day," Mike said awkwardly.

"You really did," Sarah added. "You have no idea how ruthless he can be with those types of encounters in the city streets. Just won't have it."

"Take care, you two, and thanks again! Maybe I'll see you guys around." Frank turned and headed to the door, thinking, *What are these dreams they were talking about?* He overheard Mike and Sarah's conversation about their dreams and a man in black named Mordecai.

Frank walked out of the Moon Rock with a strange feeling he'd be seeing those two again.

CHAPTER 15

Sarah nodded toward the two men leaving the café. "You were nice to those men today."

"Huh?" Mike looked over his shoulder as the men stepped out onto the sidewalk. "Yeah, so?"

"So that's what I'm talking about. The way you treated those men today was different. If I had not interfered, and made you three come to the café instead of staying out there in the street bickering, would things have ended the same way? Be honest."

"Probably not," Mike admitted. "In fact, I was about to come down on them pretty hard when you got there."

"See? That's what I'm talking about. It's about what you haven't done. Typically, I would have never interfered in your business, and you would have never let those guys get off that easy. Today, we both did things we would not normally do, and the outcome was amazing."

"I hear you, Sarah, but what does that have to do with the dream we've been having?"

"I don't know. Maybe nothing, or maybe everything. My thoughts last night, the prayers and now this today. None of it would've happened if we weren't having these dreams. Maybe the dream is a kind of metaphor."

"Representing what exactly?"

"It could represent our old way of life that needs to die, or that caring for others is our bridge to a new way of life. Maybe our lives don't end on that bridge. Perhaps our lives *begin* there. If we change how we're living, maybe the dreams will stop.

I don't know, I'm rambling. I'm sorry, Mike," Sarah said, holding back tears. "It's okay, Sarah. Besides, you may be onto something."

CHAPTER 16

"What? Seriously?" Sarah was surprised that Mike agreed.

"Yeah, seriously. I mean, the dreams have to mean something. We already agree that there is no way that this is a coincidence. We are having the exact same dream, from a different perspective, but it is the same dream. Not to mention the fact that it started at the same time for both of us, and that we are having it every night. Right now, your theory is the only one we have."

"Thanks, Mike. Who knows? If we change for the better, what's the worst that could happen? We'll actually impact other people in a positive way, and just maybe these dreams will stop. I don't see the harm in trying." Sarah noticed Mike was grinning. "Did I say something funny?" she asked suspiciously.

"No, not at all. I was just thinking that you sound more like a life coach right now than you do a waitress. You're a deep thinker, Sarah."

"Well, I don't know about all of that, but I do know I want some answers."

"I understand," Mike said, his expression softening. "We will find those answers. I promise."

Sarah smiled. "I believe that we will too. I just want my life to be about more than it is currently. I'm happy I have a job, I love my girls more than my own life, but I feel there has to be more, you know? Something bigger and more important than just me. I don't want my life to come to an end, whether on a bridge or someplace else, before I can make a difference in the world. There are people out there just like us. People who are looking for answers, love, and a little kindness. Like those two men this morning. I'm pretty sure they're having a much better day today than they would have had you not been kind to them."

"Yeah, I guess you're right. That's why I became a cop in the first place. I grew up watching how my dad helped people. Not just fellow officers, which he did, but even people who were frequent visitors to the jail. I lost count of how many times he would walk into a cell, find a familiar face, and talk to them about why they were back. I know for sure he made a difference. I wanted to be like that too, so I became a cop. I've kind of strayed away from that over the years. I let things get to me, especially Dad's death. I guess it made me a little jaded."

Mike cleared his throat, obviously moved by the memory of his father. "Thanks for the reminder. I know that part of me is still there. I need to strip away the layers of garbage. I've buried it and need to figure out how to move forward."

CHAPTER 17

Sarah paused before answering. The death of Mike's father was a sensitive subject, and she wanted to choose her words carefully.

"Mike, I believe your dad would be very proud of the man you have become. You're a good man and a good cop too. It's not surprising that his death, and the way he died, affected you in a powerful way. You can still honor his memory by being the man, and police officer, that you always wanted to be. It isn't too late."

"You're right. I guess the hardest part is letting go of the anger I have toward the man who killed dad. I wanted that man to suffer. I wanted him to die too."

"I completely understand. I'm not sure this will help, but I think that forgiving someone isn't about what it does for them, it's about what it does for you. Think about it. All the anger you carry, has it affected that man in any way? I know he got life in prison, but he would have had that anyway, right? If you refuse to let your anger go, you're in prison just as much as the man who killed your father."

Mike leaned back, took a deep breath, and released it slowly. "I hear you, Sarah. Easier said than done, but I hear you."

"Believe me, I know it isn't easy." Sarah's gaze fell to the table. "I'm talking to you as if I have it all together, but the reality is, I'm a complete mess."

"What do you mean?" Mike asked, his tone indicating concern.

"I mean I'm talking to you about forgiveness, and I know I haven't forgiven Steven for walking out on me and the girls. All of these years later, and he has never helped in any way.

He has never called to ask about the girls. Never contributed one cent to help out either. You've hated that man for killing your father, and I have hated Steven for abandoning me."

Mike reached across the table and took Sarah's hand. "I guess we both have some work to do. How does that old saying go? 'Let go and let God' or something like that?"

Sarah squeezed Mike's hand. "That sounds about right. Since when did you become so philosophical?"

Mike laughed. "What do you mean? Don't you know I'm the Socrates of the NYPD?"

"Oh, okay. Sure you are." Sarah laughed. It felt good to lighten the mood.

"Time to get back to work." Mike slid out of the booth. "I've enjoyed our talk today. Even if we haven't figured out why we're having these dreams, at least we've accomplished something. If we can let go of the past, and think about others at least as much as we think about ourselves, we'll both live happier lives."

"Amen to that." Sarah felt as if a weight had been lifted from her heart. "I could use a little more happiness in my life."

CHAPTER 18

Sarah woke up shaking and chilled to the bone. Once again, she was covered in a cold sweat and her heart was racing. She glanced at the clock on her nightstand. It was 2 a.m.

No! Please, no.

Sarah had hoped that after her conversation with Mike the day before, the dreams would stop. Instead of stopping, they had become more intense and realistic. She simply could not go on like this.

In a few hours, she would call Liz at the Moon Rock and let her know she would be taking a personal day. Then she would contact Mike and arrange a meeting somewhere besides the café. They needed to be able to talk without distractions or interruption. She hoped Mike could get away long enough to meet with her.

Sarah tried to go back to sleep, but was unsuccessful. She tossed and turned for another three hours before eventually giving up. She got coffee, showered, then made the call to Liz. Afterwards, she called Mike and he agreed to meet her at Central Park around noon. It turned out he'd taken the day off as well.

Sarah got to the park thirty minutes early, and sat down on

the bench where she had arranged to meet Mike. Less than ten minutes later, Mike arrived and sat next to her. Neither of them seemed to want to open the conversation, and they sat there without speaking for what felt like a full minute.

Mike finally broke the silence. "So, how'd you sleep?"

"Is that supposed to be funny?" Sarah quipped.

"No, not really."

"If anything, it was worse last night. It's getting harder to pull myself out of the dream, and to make matters worse, I'm actually feeling physical pain. Before, I just knew I was injured. Now I'm beginning to feel it. I don't know how much longer I can deal with this, Mike."

"I hear you. Last night was worse for me too. I don't get it. I was hoping that, somehow, things would improve. I felt good after our conversation yesterday, like we had made some progress, but now I just don't know."

"I feel the same way. I really believed we had a breakthrough yesterday, and I thought things would get better, not worse. I thought God was answering my prayers, and now I don't know what to think."

"I know." Mike ran his fingers through his hair. "I keep thinking about this guy Mordecai. It feels like I should know him, but I'm sure I don't."

Sarah stared at the ground. "So what do we do now?"

"I can tell you what we're not going to do, and that's give up. We'll find our way through this."

"I hope you're right." Sarah sighed.

"One thing that I think we can both agree on is what we talked about yesterday at Moon Rock. No matter what the explanation is for us having these dreams, we both need to change our outlook, let go of the past, and do more for others. The way I see it, we can't go wrong by doing those things. Like you said, those are things we have not been doing, so maybe doing them will bring about a change."

"You're right, of course." Sarah nodded her agreement. "We just came to that realization twenty-four hours ago, so it makes sense to give it more time. We'll both begin making changes in our lives and see where that leads us."

"Sounds like a plan. Speaking of changes, you mentioned something yesterday that I was unaware of, and I would like to see change."

Sarah eyed Mike curiously. "Okay, and what was that?"

"You said that Steven had never contributed financially to the raising of your daughters. I wish you had told me."

"What would have been the point? You have enough of your own problems to deal with."

"The point," Mike said emphatically, "is that I am your friend and I care about you."

"I know, Mike, and I appreciate it. I really do. To be honest, I thought about going after him, at least in the beginning. I was an emotional train wreck at the time and kept putting it off. After a while I lost all contact with him and felt it was too late. Steven never cared and he never will."

"I guess that's true, but you could still use the money for your girls, right?"

"Definitely, but it's been so long now I wouldn't know where to start. Besides, I don't have the money to hire a lawyer anyway."

"I know of a law firm that our department calls on sometimes to assist with certain domestic issues. One of the lawyers over there even had the nickname 'Mr. Pro Bono.' I can give you their number if you want."

"I don't know. Which law firm is it? Are they in Manhattan?"

"It's a small firm called Jones, Buchanan, and Williams. They're located in Brooklyn and—"

"What?" Sarah was dumbfounded. "Are you serious Mike?

Brooklyn?"

"Damn. I wasn't thinking Sarah. I'm exhausted and I didn't make the connection."

"Well, there's no way I'm going to Brooklyn. I don't care if their services are free. I am not going across that bridge."

CHAPTER 19

Since the dreams began, Beth found herself working late into the night on a regular basis. She wasn't a workaholic, but she knew what awaited her if she went home to sleep. Subconsciously, she hoped that her exhaustion would somehow keep the dreams from returning, but the attempt proved futile.

Each night her dream became more intense and real. She would awaken with her eyes still burning from the fumes, trapped inside the cab, and the mysterious man calling her name.

Mordecai.

Beth had no idea how she knew his name, but she did. Something else that baffled her was the fact that, in the dream, she was in a cab. When she needed transportation she used the car belonging to the firm. She had no need of a taxi service. It didn't make sense. Of course, nothing about the dream made any sense.

Arriving home at 1 a.m., Beth was exhausted and longed for a good night's sleep that she knew wouldn't come. The long days and restless nights were wearing her down.

She removed her clothes and crawled into bed. She resisted

the urge to pull the covers up over her head and hide like a frightened child. Instead, she lay on her back and stared up at the ceiling. Her thoughts drifted to her work. She no longer enjoyed it as she had in the past. When she graduated law school, she had been on top of the world. She was passionate about doing the right thing and making a difference in the world. She was going to use her career in law to do good and to help people.

Now, all she cared about was winning and moving on to the next case.

What's happened to me?

Somewhere along the path she had lost her way. She wondered what Uncle Henry would think of her now. She rolled onto her side and looked at the picture frame on her nightstand. It was a picture of her and her uncle the day she graduated from law school. She loved that picture and the way it made her feel when she looked at it. She missed him and would give anything to be able to talk to him now. He would know just what to say to help her get back on track, and rid herself of the nightmares.

Tears streamed down Beth's face. It had been seven years since her uncle had been killed by a drunk driver. Her life changed that day, and not for the better. She hated the man who had taken her uncle from her, and over time that hate turned to bitterness. She grabbed the picture frame and looked at the happy woman in the photograph. She barely recognized her.

If I could only go back and be that woman again.

Beth remembered clearly the words her uncle had spoken to her that day. He told her, "Beth, you just do what you know to be right, and know that God is with you every step of the way. If you can remember that, then you'll be able to get through any adversity."

She gripped the picture frame tightly and held it to her chest.

God, are you really there? Uncle Henry said you would always be with me, but I just don't know. I'm sorry. If you hear me, would you please show me the way out of this mess.

Beth was surprised at herself. She had not uttered a word in prayer for years, yet she had just prayed. It caused her to feel a bit lighter, and though she still did not have any answers, she felt more at peace. Her eyelids heavy, she was reluctant to give into sleep.

She wanted to explore her feelings, maybe pray once again, but she finally succumbed to sleep.

A few hours later, Beth was back on the Brooklyn Bridge. Her throat was burning and her eyes watered from the smoke and fumes. She was in the cab, trying to get the door open, but to no avail. Standing outside the cab was Mordecai, speaking to her in his calm voice and telling her it would be okay.

She could see Manhattan in the distance, and knew she must had been on her way there. She had no idea why. The smoke thickened and she was gasping for air.

Beth's eyes flew open wide. She sat straight up in bed, still clutching the picture frame. Tears again filled her eyes. She looked down at the photograph and into her uncle's eyes. Her heart slowed its pace and her breathing returned to normal. She felt a strange sensation rush over her, and could not tear her eyes away from the picture. It dawned on her what she was feeling, though she could not explain why she was feeling it at that moment. It had been so long that, at first, she did not recognize it for what it was.

It was hope.

CHAPTER 20

Frank stared up at the red light through the windshield of his cab, but he wasn't seeing the light. In his mind he was looking at Mordecai walking toward his cab. He could smell the smoke and hear the cries of the lady in the back seat.

The dreams were becoming more vivid each night, and were now invading his thoughts during the day. It was becoming too much.

Something's got to give. I can't do this.

The sound of a car horn snapped him out of his thoughts. The light had turned green. As he pulled away from the light, his thoughts focused on the man in his dreams. Who was Mordecai anyway? He could not answer that question. In fact, he wasn't sure how he even knew the man's name.

Frank had never been one to have dreams while he slept, or at least he did not remember them if he did. He wished he could say the same about the dream that now owned his nights. They were becoming so realistic that he was having trouble separating them from reality.

He needed answers and he could only think of one place to start asking questions. The Moon Rock Café.

That fiery little waitress was talking to that policeman about a dream. I know what I heard. Maybe she can shed some light on all of this.

CHAPTER 21

The sweat stung George's eyes, causing him to flash back to the dream he had again the night before. It seemed that more and more of his waking hours were spent reliving that dream.

I'm getting sick of this.

Standing there, in the midst of rubble that used to be a beautiful old building, he took a long look around. He was surrounded by the ruins of things that once mattered, but now was cared about by no one.

What a waste.

George took a sip of his energy drink, then sat down on a pile of debris. Tearing down old things and starting over was what his job was all about. He knew there was a metaphor about life in there somewhere, but let the thought pass. He did not have time to venture down that road, and he knew that was a big part of his problem. He did not have much time for anything. His life revolved around his job, going to the gym, and sleep, though he was not getting much sleep anymore.

For too long he had pushed everything and everyone out of his life. If he was honest with himself, he'd admit that it wasn't that he did not have time, he simply did not make the time. It was a rut he had been in for years, and now it felt normal. The dreams that returned every night had upset his comfortable, isolated world and caused him to think in ways he had abandoned long ago.

George removed his hard hat, and ran his fingers through his hair. He closed his eyes and let the light breeze cool his sweaty brow. The image of Mordecai flashed in his mind, reaching out to him on the ledge of the bridge, and speaking in a low, calm voice. George opened his eyes, half expecting Mordecai to still be standing in front of him.

I have got to get a grip.

George was mystified how he knew the man's name. He did not remember hearing it in the dream. He just knew.

Here he was, a grown man, having nightmares. It reminded him of being a young boy and waking up in the night terrified. His mom would hear his cries and come to his rescue. She would tell him that God wouldn't let anything happen to him. He could hear her voice in his mind: *George, you're chosen, chosen by God to do great things. God won't let anything happen to you. Now, go back to sleep.*

Chosen for what, Mom? Surely this is not it.

The dreams were making him crazy. For the first time in a while, he wished for someone to talk to. He remembered the waitress at the Moon Rock Café and wondered if she had really been talking about the same dream. Should he go there and try to talk to her? Would she think he was out of his mind?

Probably. He was beginning to think so too, so what did he have to lose?

CHAPTER 22

Sarah twirled her hair with her finger, thinking about what to do next. "I think we should go back to the conversation we had yesterday."

"Okay. What about it?" Mike leaned back on the park bench.

"We both felt like we hit upon something, like we had a breakthrough or something. I know for sure that I felt so much better after our talk, and I'm pretty sure you did too."

Mike nodded.

"Okay, good," Sarah continued. "Naturally, we were both upset that we had the dream again last night, but it's only been one day since we had our breakthrough. I mean, we talked about it, but we haven't begun living differently yet. The more I think about it, the more convinced I become that the key is for us to put into action everything we talked about."

"That makes sense," Mike agreed. "Like you said about those two guys who had been arguing on the street. Typically, I would have laid the law down on them pretty hard and called it a day. I handled it differently, for whatever reason, and the end result was pretty amazing. Those men left on friendly terms, and I felt pretty good about it. Very good actually. Who knows, maybe if we have more days like that, things will begin to change for us."

"Yes, exactly!" Sarah was excited that Mike seemed to be coming around. "I'm going to start by letting go of my anger toward Steven. I may still consider trying to get some back child support, for the girls' sake, but I'm through with carrying around all the hate. And I am still not going to Brooklyn!"

Mike chuckled. "I don't blame you. I admire what you're doing, Sarah. I know it won't be easy. I'm going to try to follow your example and ditch the hate I've been carrying for the man who murdered my dad. It will probably be the hardest thing I've ever done, but just saying it out loud feels pretty liberating. Ever since Dad was killed, I've been mad at most everyone, even God."

"God?" Sarah raised her eyebrows. "Since when does God enter into your mind?"

"Yeah, yeah," Mike said. "You just might be surprised at the things I think about. I think the bottom line here is that we both want to live our lives differently."

"Well said, and I wholeheartedly agree. In whatever role we play, whether it's a waitress, policeman, or whatever we do in the future. We will both dump the garbage from our past and let go of what's been holding us down. That way, dreams or no dreams, we will be happier, better people."

"I think you are right, Sarah." Mike's tone was hopeful. "If we're happy, maybe we can help make others happy too. At the very least, it will mean that the only time we're living a nightmare is when we're asleep."

CHAPTER 23

George downed the last of his energy drink, stretched his sore muscles, and prepared to get back to work. His heart was not in it, so he was in no rush. What he needed was something to do that actually meant something. He tried to push thoughts of his dreams out of his mind. Mordecai, the pileup and the cries for help. It all seemed so real and left him feeling depressed and alone.

How did my life become so pointless?

He peered through the window of the demolished building to the billboard across the street. It was an advertisement for Habitat for Humanity. The sign said that one could bring in old doors, windows, or any unused building materials and they would be used to build houses for homeless families.

George stood frozen, his eyes fixed on the billboard. A wave of emotion washed over him. He felt hope and a sense of purpose for the first time in a very long time.

It has been, literally, right in front of me all of this time.

How long had he been drifting through life without a sense of meaning and purpose? He had been on autopilot, and merely going through the motions. It never occurred to him that the skills he had acquired through his job could be put to use helping others.

How have I not seen this before now?

He took in his surroundings with different eyes. No longer did he see only refuse and waste. Now, he also saw opportunity. From where he stood he spotted a perfectly good door, a chair, and even a couple of windows.

George threw himself into his work with renewed vigor. Never had he been so excited to be demolishing a building. As he worked he looked for anything that could be salvaged, being careful to not to damage anything that could be used to build a home for someone in need. He stockpiled all of his finds in one area, and would haul them away after he got off work. He couldn't explain why he'd experienced such a sudden change in his attitude. But it felt right, so he didn't question it.

Maybe Mom was right. Maybe I am chosen, and this is how I can make a difference.

George wasn't sure that his new mission had anything to do with his nightmares, or if they would ever stop. All he knew for certain was that what he was doing at that moment was right, and he would do it with all of his heart. It was a start, and for now, that was enough.

CHAPTER 24

Beth was the first to arrive at the firm. She liked being the first person in the office and enjoyed the morning quiet time. It had been a long night, but she felt strangely refreshed and equipped with new hope.

She put on a pot of coffee and sat down in her chair. The phone on her desk indicated she had voicemails, and a stack of files on her desk awaited her attention. Beth got a cup of coffee and returned to her desk. She kicked off her shoes, leaned back in her chair, and cradled the warm mug in her hands. The files and voicemails could wait.

Beth was not the sentimental type, but when it came to her uncle Henry, it was a different story. She remembered how she felt the night before, after her nightmare, when she looked at the photograph of her and her uncle. She had gazed into his eyes and was overcome with peace and a sense of hope, neither of which she had experienced in quite some time. She had always had a special connection to her uncle, but last night's experience was different. It was like he was trying to tell her something.

She repeated in her mind again the advice her uncle had given her on graduation day. *Beth, you just do what you know to be right, and know that God is with you every step of the way.*

Do what is right. Do I even know what that is anymore?

Thoughts of her uncle caused her to remember something. The firm had dedicated an entire wall in honor of her uncle. On the wall were various plaques, diplomas, photographs, and letters of commendation. How many times had she walked by that wall, unnoticing, on the way to her office? She pushed back her chair and, in her stocking feet, walked out of her office and down the hall. Reverently, she approached the wall, taking in all of the memorabilia that bore witness to a life spent in service to others. This man was the reason she had chosen to be an attorney. His example, especially the way he treated others, was the single greatest influence upon her decision to attend law school. She had wanted to be like him, and for her life to be as impactful as his had been.

What happened to me?

Of course, she knew the answer to that question. Her eyes continued to scan the wall until they landed on a letter her uncle had received from the mayor of Syracuse, New York. Uncle Henry had helped so many less fortunate people over the years that he soon earned the moniker Mr. Pro Bono. The letter accompanied a plaque inscribed with the well-deserved moniker, which in Latin meant "for the public good." Beth read the letter through tear-filled eyes.

Dear Mr. Buchanan,

I am honored to write you this letter, and to have had the privilege of meeting you in person at several city hall meetings. It has been amazing to watch your career flourish and to see you become one of our city's most esteemed attorneys. In a field of endeavor where one's honesty and integrity are often questioned, you have forever remained beyond reproach.

It is a rare and wonderful thing to find a human being

of your caliber, and one filled with compassion for those in need. For all of the years of faithful service to your fellow man, and to the city of Syracuse, we present to you this plaque. Please accept it along with our deepest gratitude.

Joseph W. Barnett
Mayor, Syracuse, New York

Beth wiped the tears from her eyes. Others were beginning to arrive at the firm and she did not want to be seen crying in the hallway. She retreated to her office and closed the door. She sat down at her desk and slipped her shoes on. She needed a few minutes to regain her composure before beginning her work day.

Reminiscing about Uncle Henry and the life he had led reminded her of the person she had set out to become. It amazed her that after all of these years, merely looking into his eyes in that photograph could have such a powerful impact on her. Up until the day he was killed, he had never wavered from helping anyone who crossed his path. He spent countless hours volunteering his services to those who were in desperate need, but could not pay. The only thing he ever asked of those he helped was to pay it forward.

Beth decided she was done living the way she had for the last several years. The hate and bitterness had hardened her heart, and she had turned her back on the very ideals passed to her by Uncle Henry. It was time to let go of the past and move forward.

Pay it forward, it is. Just like Uncle Henry would want me to do.

CHAPTER 25

Frank sat in his cab, watching the people on the sidewalk run for shelter from the rain. He was running on almost no sleep, thanks to the nightmares that would not go away. Rainy days made him irritable. It made it a pain to drive in the city, and people drove like idiots. He drummed his fingers on the steering wheel, keeping time with the windshield wipers as they struggled against the downpour. He was parked at the curb, in front of a hotel, waiting for his next fare. Now that the storm had begun, and it was getting dark, it was only a matter of time.

Frank wondered how many hours of his life had been spent waiting.

Waiting for what? A few dollars from the next fare?

He wasn't complaining. He liked being a cab driver, and it had made him a living for many years. There were days when he felt like he should be doing more with his life, something more fulfilling and meaningful. Today was one of those days.

Someone on the sidewalk caught his attention. He squinted through the pounding rain and saw a young woman pushing a stroller down the sidewalk. Her head was down and her shoulders were hunched against the rain. Frank could see she had removed her raincoat and had draped it haphazardly over the stroller.

What the hell?

Frank rolled down the passenger side window and called out to the lady, "Hey! Get in!" he nodded toward the back door of the cab.

"I don't have any money, but thank you." She replied, water streaming down her face.

Frank jumped out of the cab and ran around the car to where she was standing. "Look, just get in the cab. This one is on me, okay?"

Frank snatched open the rear door and motioned for the woman to get in. The woman grabbed her baby from the stroller, and jumped into the back seat. Frank popped open the trunk and stored the stroller inside. He jumped back into his cab and turned to face the lady in the back. "Where do you need to go?" he asked.

The woman thanked him again and told him her address. It was not far away, which made Frank happy. He did not like having a baby in his cab that was not fastened securely in a car seat. Fortunately, he would be able to take side streets to get where he was going. He would take it slow and easy.

What the hell are you doing?

Frank was surprised at himself. When he had spotted the young woman on the sidewalk, something came over him. He couldn't sit there and do nothing. His reaction was almost automatic. It was obvious what he had to do and he did not stop to think about it. Now that he had done it, he found himself feeling pretty good. Helping the young woman and her baby had shifted his mood. He glanced up in the rearview mirror and saw he was smiling. The woman in the back seat smiled back at him.

In thirty-two years of being a cab driver, not once had Frank given a free ride to anyone. Now that he had, he was experiencing emotions that had long been buried. He felt light, even happy, and was humming along to the song on the radio. He no longer cared that it was raining, and had not yelled at any other driver since leaving the hotel.

He arrived at the address and helped the woman and her baby exit the cab. She extended her hand and thanked him again. Her warm smile and soft hand melted Frank's heart.

He watched as she walked up the steps into her home.

Frank climbed back into his cab. Tears were welling up in his eyes. He had just done something for someone and had asked for nothing in return. In fact, the woman had no way to pay him even if he had insisted. It was an act of kindness and generosity, and he could not remember the last time he had done such a thing. He could not hold back the tears. He gripped the steering wheel and let himself cry. He felt as though he was releasing stress, bitterness, and anger that he had been carrying for years. He found it fascinating that he was not the least bit sad. If anything, he was extremely happy. The rain continued to fall, but he felt as though the clouds had parted, and the sun was beaming onto his face.

I suppose no one sets out to become callused. It has been too many years.

Frank wondered if the lack of sleep had in any way contributed to what happened. He certainly had not been himself since the dreams began a few weeks ago.

You know what? I don't care why it happened. I'm just glad it did.

He turned up the radio and drove back toward the hotel. He was actually looking forward to his next fare.

CHAPTER 26

Sarah lay in her bed, exhausted but wide awake. Her girls were tucked in for the night. She kept going over in her head everything that she had talked about with Mike when they met at the park. Had they reached a conclusion, or merely a course of action? Since they had not solved the riddle of why they were having these dreams, she presumed it was the latter. They both agreed to make significant changes in their lives, and to seek out ways to help others.

Who knows? Maybe by taking our eyes off of ourselves, things will change for us too. Perhaps the nightmares will fade away.

Sarah felt that it was easier for Mike to find ways to help others than it was for her. After all, Mike was a police officer and she was only a waitress. What could she possibly do? Mike could use his position and influence in a number of ways, but how could she make a difference?

She tossed and turned, unable to sleep, as if she wanted to anyway. Sleep no longer meant rest, it meant the terrifying dream would return. Still, she did not want to close her eyes until she had some idea of what she could do to change her life. Then, a thought began to take shape in her mind.

What if it's not so much about how I can change my life, but more about what I can do to change the lives of other people?

"Okay, so I am a waitress."

Lord, please. Show me what I can do to change the lives of others.

She could not fight her exhaustion any longer. Her eyelids grew heavy and she drifted off to sleep, and returned to the Brooklyn Bridge.

Sarah was busy cleaning off tables, but her mind had picked up right where it had left off the night before. She was determined to become the kind of person that made a positive impact in the lives of others. She just was not sure how to begin. She picked up a load of dirty dishes and ran them back to the kitchen. She was racking the dirty dishes into the dishwasher when she heard the door chime. Hoping it was Mike, she rushed back into the seating area. Instead of Mike, she saw another face that looked familiar. It was the cab driver from the other day.

What is he doing here?

The man was not a regular, and she did not remember him being in the café before until the day she had interfered in the argument he was having with a construction worker. Sarah assumed he must be here looking for Mike.

"Officer Nelson isn't here," she said flatly.

"Excuse me, ma'am, but I'm not looking for the police officer. I came to talk to you."

Sarah was caught off guard. "Me? Why do you want to talk to me?"

The man winced.

Sarah realized she must have sounded harsh. "Forgive me. I didn't mean to sound rude. Remind me of your name?"

"Frank. My name is Frank," he replied softly.

Sarah extended her hand. "Hello, Frank. My name is Sarah. Would you like to have a seat?" She gestured toward a table.

Frank took a seat at the table while Sarah grabbed him a cup of coffee. She regretted the way she had reacted toward Frank. It seemed that her demeanor had flipped back to cynical, which had been her default for the past few years. She was grateful she was now self-aware enough to realize it, and to make a change.

Sarah put the full mug on the table and sat across from Frank. "What brings you to the Moon Rock today?" she asked, careful to use a friendly tone.

Frank paused a moment before answering. "Thank you for taking the time to talk with me. I know you're working so I won't keep you long. I wanted to ask you about the discussion you were having with the policeman the other day. I didn't purposely eavesdrop, but I couldn't help but overhear you mention something about a dream and a man named Mordecai. I've been having dreams too, every night, and there's a man with the same name who speaks to me. I need to know what it means."

Sarah didn't know what to say, or where to begin. She wasn't sure what she had expected, but this was not it. A chill ran over her body.

How is this possible?

Frank reached across the table and touched Sarah's hand. "I'm sorry. I didn't mean to upset you."

"No, it's okay." Sarah hoped her voice sounded more composed than she felt. "You just caught me by surprise, that's all."

"I understand, believe me," Frank said. "So, I take it I was right. You and the policeman, I can't recall his name, have been having a similar dream?"

"His name is Mike, and it seems you could be right. Can you tell me more about the dream you've been having?" Sarah had conflicting feelings about hearing him out. Part of her did not want to hear what Frank was about to say, but another part of her had to know.

Frank took a deep breath and released it slowly. "It started about a month ago. In fact, it was exactly thirty-two days ago. I keep a notepad by my bed and I've kept track." He paused, as if searching for the right words.

Sarah could see he was in turmoil. "Frank, I know how hard this is for you to talk about, believe me. I have carried the same burden for weeks. Talking to Mike has been the only thing keeping me from losing my mind. So, talk to me. It will help you feel better, I promise." She smiled.

"Okay," Frank continued. "Like I said, it started thirty-two days ago. I'm driving my cab across the Brooklyn Bridge. That in itself is strange because in all of my twenty-two years of driving a cab, I have never operated in Brooklyn. Until recently, that is. I'll tell you about that later. Anyway, I'm involved in a huge accident. Multiple cars and the entire bridge is shut down. There's smoke, fumes and I can hear people crying for help. I have a fare in the back and we're both trapped in my cab and unable to get out. Then, out of nowhere comes this guy dressed in black. He's clean and uninjured, so I know he can't be one of the victims. He walks up to my cab and starts talking to me. He keeps telling me to open the door and starts tugging on the door handle. Somehow, I know his name is Mordecai even though I'm sure he never tells me that in my dream. That's usually when I wake up with my heart beating out of my chest. It's getting worse too. Now, even after I wake up, I swear I can still smell the fumes and hear people crying for help."

"You just described, almost verbatim, the dream I have been having. Mike too. Your perspective is different, meaning you're in the cab, while Mike is in his police car and I'm in a city bus. Other than that, it's the same dream. This is impossible."

Frank laughed dryly. "Well, it may be impossible, but that doesn't change the fact that it's really happening. What do you and Mike think it means? Are we all going crazy?"

"I have no idea what it means and neither does Mike. We have talked about it several times, and we can't make sense out of it. I don't believe we are all going crazy, but at the same time, I don't know what any of this means."

Frank sipped his coffee as if deep in thought. "You know what else is strange? In the midst of all of this, something odd happened to me yesterday."

"What do you mean?"

"I was waiting for a fare outside of a hotel yesterday. It was pouring down rain and I was lost in my own thoughts. I do that sometimes. I get to wondering what I'm doing with my life and how I feel like I've wasted so many years. Feeling sorry for myself, I guess, or maybe it's just a midlife crisis. Who knows?"

"So what happened?" Sarah was anxious to hear the rest of the story.

"For some reason, a lady on the sidewalk got my attention. She was walking, head down and pushing a stroller. She had a raincoat but had taken it off and draped over her baby in the stroller. It's hard to explain, but something came over me. I couldn't stand the thought of this woman and her baby being caught out in the rain. I rolled down the window and asked her to get in the cab. She said something about not having any money, and started to move on. Without thinking, I jumped out of the cab and asked her to please get in the cab. I told her the ride was on me."

"How sweet! That was such a nice thing to do."

"I know, and that's what I meant when I said something strange happened. I hate to admit it, but that's not the kind of man I am, or at least not for many years. I've pretty much been a loner and wrapped up in my own life. It's sad, I know, but I haven't really thought about other people that much. Not for a long time. Anyway, after I dropped her off at her home, I sat in my cab and cried like a baby. Since then, I feel different. I look in the mirror and I don't even recognize the man staring back at me. I can't explain it, but I'm different. Something's changed. My whole life has been turned upside down, and it all started with those damn dreams."

Sarah was amazed. Here was a man that she did not know, yet he was experiencing the same dreams and life-altering transformation as she and Mike. Was all of it somehow connected? If so, how?

"Frank, I don't know what to say. I could say I'm completely blown away, but that would be the understatement of the year. Everything you are describing, from the dreams to your own personal transformation, is exactly what me and Mike have been going through. In fact, the only conclusion we have come to out of all of this is that our lives need to change. Like you, we both had become wrapped up in our own little world, and had shut out everyone else. What that has to do with the nightmares, we have no clue. We're hoping that, by changing how we live, that the dreams will stop. If not, then at least we'll be happier while we're awake."

Frank smiled. "Well, there certainly has to be more to life than what I've been doing. I guess I agree with you and Mike. Other than the nightmares, I feel much better about life. Maybe these dreams are some kind of wake-up call."

Sarah nodded. "They have certainly gotten our attention, so maybe you're right."

CHAPTER 27

"For the public good."

Beth kept repeating that softly to herself. Her uncle Henry had lived by that motto for his entire life. He had inspired her more than any other person she had ever known. It pained her to admit it, but somewhere along the way, she had stepped off the path. She used to be full of life and had a heart for helping others. She had buried all of that, along with her uncle, years ago.

No more. I will not live like that any longer.

For the first time in years, Beth felt hope again. It was like her eyes had been opened, and could finally see the person she had become. It horrified her. Whatever it took, she would change, and nothing would stop her. Not even the terrifying dreams in the night.

Who knows? If I change, maybe the dreams will stop.

There was a time when she had worked hard to emulate her uncle and the way he lived. Uncle Henry loved people and loved helping people. Everything he did, he did with passion and joy. He used his position as an attorney for good, and not only for gain.

Some people were impressed with one's family name, or position in life, but not Uncle Henry. He treated everyone with the same respect and compassion. That was his legacy, and she would pick up where he left off.

CHAPTER 28

Still sitting at the Moon Rock, Frank was lost in his own thoughts, contemplating everything he and Sarah had shared with each other.

"I have an idea," Sarah said, breaking their silence. "Would you be up for meeting together with me and Mike?"

Frank nodded enthusiastically. "Yes! Absolutely. Just tell me when and where."

"How about this Friday around 10 p.m.? We can meet here. Things are usually pretty slow around that time, and we should be able to talk."

"Sounds good to me. Maybe between the three of us we can figure something out."

"It's certainly worth a try," Sarah agreed.

They exchanged phone numbers, just in case, and Frank got up to leave. He paused at the door, then looked back at Sarah, who was still seated at the table. "Thank you again. I was about to say, 'You have no idea how much this means to me,' but I think you do."

Sarah smiled. "I'll see you on Friday. Have a great day!"

Frank walked back to his cab and climbed inside. He put the key in the ignition and started the engine. He made a new friend today, and that made him happy.

I think I could get used to this.

There was so much going on in his life, but instead of feeling overwhelmed, he felt grateful. He was grateful for the lady and baby he had helped, and grateful he had met Sarah and Mike.

Hmm. I'm beginning to think our meeting wasn't an accident.

CHAPTER 29

Sarah wiped down the table where she and Frank had been sitting. Her mind was reeling and her body buzzed with new energy. The thought that there was yet another person who was experiencing the same dream gave her hope. It all had to mean something.

I cannot wait to tell Mike. This is mind-blowing.

It was also interesting that the three of them shared something else in common. They had all been undergoing some kind of change. Each of them had been living lives that were sheltered from other people. Now, that seemed to be changing. They were all beginning to focus on helping others. It was a common theme and, as far as Sarah was concerned, it was beyond coincidence.

This definitely has to mean something.

Sarah had endured weeks of nightmares, had her eyes opened to the miserable way she had been living her life, yet she was filled with hope and happiness.

She looked around the café as if she was seeing it, and the people, for the first time.

It's been right in front of me all this time.

Every day at the café she encountered dozens of people. She could now see that each interaction was an opportunity to make an impact on someone's life. Maybe it was just a smile, or a kind word, but she could make a difference. She would serve more than just drinks and food, she would serve joy and compassion.

God, if you're there and you hear me, show me how I can help these people. Show me how I can, in some way, make their lives better. I know I'm here for a reason.

The café door chimed, signaling the end of her prayer. She glanced at the door with expectation, and into the eyes of a stranger with a grim expression. She smiled warmly and watched with joy as the stranger's face brightened with a smile of their own.

Thank you.

CHAPTER 30

Beth felt as though she had been given a second chance at life. The wall that the firm had dedicated in honor of her uncle Henry provided concrete reminders of the person she had set out to be. Her uncle had been the inspiration back then, and he was her source of inspiration now. Her eyes filled with joyful tears.

How could I not see this before? Why am I seeing it now?

The past month had been one of the most difficult months of her life. The dreams had been pushing her to the edges of her sanity, and she was ill-equipped to deal with it. It did not make sense to her, but the dreams, in some way, had caused her to rethink everything about her life. The dreams were terrifying, but here she was now, filled with joy and hope. It no longer mattered to her how she spent her nights, she would focus on spending her days living the legacy left to her by her dear uncle.

Whatever horrors I endure in the night will be wiped away by my love for others during the day. Those dreams will not hold me prisoner any longer.

Beth spun in her desk chair 360 degrees like a child on a merry-go-round. She felt free. She stopped spinning and eyed the stack of files on her desk. The site of them no longer felt overwhelming. In fact, she looked forward to working on them. She was also looking forward to working with the people those files represented. She knew already that there were at least three clients in that stack who could not afford her services. Just a few days before, she had decided to call those clients and let them know she would not take their case. Now, she decided she was contact those clients first, and tell them she would happily help them.

Thank you, Uncle Henry.

CHAPTER 31

The closer Sarah got to the subway entrance, the faster she walked. By the time she got to the stairs that would take her underground, she was almost running. She was excited about getting to work and beginning a new day. At some point, she knew Mike would show up and she had a lot to tell him.

Sarah wove her way through the swarm of commuters, making a beeline for the train. In the midst of rushing crowd, just a few feet in front of her, she spotted a man with a familiar face, and dressed in black. He did not move as he looked at Sarah and smiled. She stood frozen, not believing her eyes, afraid to take another step.

Mordecai.

As suddenly as he had appeared, Mordecai was gone. Sarah frantically searched the crowd, but there was no sign of him. Am I dreaming?

Or am I really losing my mind?

Sarah stepped onto the train and the doors slid closed behind her. She grabbed a vacant seat, grateful to be sitting down. Did she hallucinate? Perhaps the lack of sleep was catching up with her. She could not bring herself to accept any other explanation.

Just when I thought this could not get any weirder.

Sarah arrived at the Moon Rock, stored her stuff in the back, and punched her time card. She said good morning to Liz, tied on her apron, and went right to work opening the café.

As she went about her duties, her mind wandered to the dream she had again the night before. Mordecai had walked to the bus and spoke to her as he had every *night for weeks.*

She remembered asking him, Am I dead?

Mordecai had smiled at her question, working to gently remove the shattered glass from her face. *You will be fine,* he answered. *It's time to cross the bridge, Sarah.*

The door chime drew her out of her daydream. It was Mike, and he was much earlier than usual.

He walked over to the counter where Sarah was working. "Can I get a cup of coffee, please? Extra strong if you have it."

"Of course," she replied. "Go sit down and I'll bring it right over."

Sarah fought the urge to rush over to Mike's booth and spill out everything that had happened since they last saw each other.

Lord, please help me be calm.

She sat the coffee on the table. "You okay, Mike? You have that look on your face again."

Mike wrapped his hands around the warm mug. "You know, I had almost got to the point where I was ready to accept all of the weird things that have been going on lately, and then it got even weirder."

The café had just opened, and was not busy, so Sarah sat down. "Funny that you say that, because I was about to tell you the same thing."

Mike raised his eyebrows. "Is that so? Well, do tell."

Sarah smiled. "You first."

Mike took a sip of the strong black coffee. "Okay, but you're not going to believe this."

"Try me," Sarah said dryly.

"Guess who showed up at the precinct yesterday, asking for me."

"I have no idea."

"Do you remember the two guys that were arguing on the street the other day? The cab driver and construction worker? I think their names were Frank and George."

Sarah felt the familiar chill run down her spine. "Yes, I remember."

"Well, the construction worker, George, walks into the front desk asking for me. I come downstairs to see what he wanted, and he starts going on about how he overheard us talking that day here in the café. He said he heard us talking about a dream, the Brooklyn Bridge and a strange man in black. I led him outside to finish the conversation. I don't need anyone at the precinct hearing about all of this. They'd have me taken in for a psych eval. I don't need that on my record."

Sarah was shocked. "Are you telling me that he is having the dream too?"

"That's exactly what I'm telling you. He went on to describe the bridge, the pileup, and even Mordecai. George thinks that he may have somehow caused the accident."

"How?"

"He said, in the dream, that he was hauling a load of scrap across the bridge, and somehow the load came off the truck and caused the accident. He said he was thrown from his truck and was laying on a ledge. Mordecai walks up and asks George to take his hand. He was pretty shaken up about it. He kept asking what you and I know about the dream."

"What did you tell him?"

"What *could* I tell him? I told him we'd been having similar dreams and that I'd get back to him. He calmed down after a few minutes and shared something else I think you'll find interesting. He said he'd been unhappy with how his life has turned out, and that it had lost its meaning. Then, he was on a job the other day and noticed a billboard across the street. It was an ad for Habitat for Humanity. He went on about how he now knows how he can help others and that life now has new meaning for him. You see a theme developing here?"

"Mike, this is incredible. If I had any doubts that these dreams have a larger purpose, I have them no longer. Especially after what I have seen and heard the past day or two."

Mike leaned over the table. "What do you mean? Has something happened?

"You could say that," Sarah said with a half smile.

Sarah told Mike about her conversation with Frank, her own revelation about how she could bring hope to others through her job, and finally about seeing Mordecai in the subway.

Sarah leaned back in the booth and sighed. "I don't know whether to believe that we are discovering what all of this is about, or if I am simply going nuts."

"I believe we're slowly finding answers, Sarah. We have to hang in there until we know for sure. Can you do that?"

"Yes. I can do that."

"Good. I guess you know what we need to do now, right?"

"I do. We have to meet with Frank and George. In fact, I have already arranged for Frank to meet us here this Friday night."

Mike chuckled. "Great minds think alike. I will get ahold of George."

CHAPTER 32

Mike sat in his car outside the precinct. He was replaying in his mind the conversation he had with Sarah the day before. He was exhausted, again, from lack of sleep. He reached up to adjust the rearview mirror and found himself staring into the eyes of Mordecai.

"What the hell?" Mike snapped his head around and looked in the back seat. There was no one there. He quickly climbed out of the car, slammed the door, and searched the interior for any sign of Mordecai.

Damn. Maybe Sarah was right. Maybe we really are going nuts.

Mike shook it off, telling himself it was the weeks of sleepless nights causing his mind to hallucinate. He slogged his way into the building, up the elevator and, finally, to his desk. He made the decision to view everything he was going through like a cop. He would look at the "facts" from the dream and see if there was any connection between them. There was the Brooklyn Bridge, the pileup, and Mordecai. All of these things were present in the dream no matter who was having it. He would start with Mordecai.

Mike switched on his computer, then went to grab a cup of coffee while it was booting up. By the time he returned, it was ready to go. He logged in to the NYPD database and decided to do a first name search for Mordecai. It wasn't exactly a common name, so he hoped to find something. He got three hits, all in the state of New York, and all three men had a record. He dug a little deeper into the records of each man and found that two of the men were dead. One was killed in prison, and the other of natural causes.

Great. Only three possibilities and already two of them are dead ends.

The last man on the list was Mordecai Thomas. Mike continued his research until he found something that sent a cold chill throughout his body. Sadly, Mordecai Thomas was also dead, but that isn't what gave him chills. Mordecai Thomas had apparently died as a result of an automobile accident, and his body had been found in the East River. He was born and raised in Brooklyn. The data base informed Mike that the files on Mordecai Thomas were in storage downstairs in the archive room.

Mike jumped up from his desk and took the elevator downstairs. He told the file clerk that he needed to look at some old files regarding a cold case. Mike signed in and entered the large file room. The room was huge, at least eight thousand square feet, and contained row after row of shelves piled high with boxes. The aisles were arranged alphabetically, and Mike had no trouble locating the correct one. He walked between two rows of shelves, scanning boxes for the right name.

It took him only a few minutes to locate the correct box. He pulled it off the shelf and sat it down on the cold concrete floor. He found only one file folder inside. It was stuffed full of papers and bound by a large rubber band. He scooped the folder out of the box, and stood up to get a better angle from the overhead light. He flipped through the file until he came across a police report of a car accident the night of Mordecai's death. As he scanned the file, an old photograph fell from the file to the floor. Mike stooped to pick up the mugshot and froze. Staring back at him from the cold concrete floor was the man who had appeared in his dreams for weeks.

It's him. It's Mordecai.

Mike retrieved the picture and carefully slid it back into the file. He scanned more papers in the folder and found some typewritten notes regarding Mordecai.

Thomas, Mordecai
White male
Height: 6'2"
Weight: 210 lbs.
Age: 37
DOB: March 4, 1946
Place of Birth: Brooklyn, New York
Date of Death: December 20
Subject's body found in the East River.
Cause of Death: Accidental
History of gang activity prior to 1978.
No record of arrests beyond 1978.
Involved with various community programs 1978–1980.

Mike didn't know what to think. No longer was Mordecai a mysterious apparition from a dream. He was, or had been, a real person. He closed the file and paced up and down the aisle, attempting to wrap his head around why this man was appearing to people in their dreams.

What the hell does he want from us?

Mike tucked the file into his waistband and hid it with his jacket. He did not need anyone asking questions about the file. He put the lid back on the box and returned the box to the shelf. He signed out with the clerk and walked out of the room.

CHAPTER 33

Beth felt like it was her first week on the job. She was meeting with a client today and found herself feeling nervous. She had met with the client before, a child custody case, and the client had run out of money. She had advised the client to settle, but called the young mother that morning to arrange a meeting. Beth knew things were different, *she* was different, and she was anxious to inform the client that she would continue to represent her pro bono. From now on, she would carry the torch passed to her by her uncle.

Later that night, as Beth crawled beneath the cold sheets of her bed, she was still smiling. Her meeting with the client had gone even better than she had expected. The look of relief and gratitude on the face of that young mother was worth far more than money. No matter what else happened, Beth knew she had made a difference that day.

Soon, Beth drifted off to sleep and found herself in an all-too-familiar place. She was on the Brooklyn Bridge, trapped in the back seat of a cab, surrounded by fumes and cries of people in distress. Mordecai was there, pulling on the door handle of the cab. She could hear the driver talking, but could not make out what he was saying.

Beth tried to free herself, but was unsuccessful. Mordecai was speaking to her as he tried to open the door.

Beth, it's Mordecai. His voice, as always, was calm and soothing.

Beth tried to answer, but the fumes and smoke had taken her breath away. The cab driver's voice began to fade, as if he were now far away.

Smoke burned her eyes and tears streamed down her face.

"Shit!" Beth bolted upright in her bed. Her breath came in short gasps.

Why? Didn't yesterday mean anything?

She was angry and scared.

Please, God. I can't take this anymore.

CHAPTER 34

Frank was approaching an intersection when he glanced to his right toward the sidewalk. There were several pedestrians waiting to cross the street, but his eyes were drawn to one man in particular. It was Mordecai, the man from his dreams, standing next to an elderly man holding a cane. Their eyes locked, and Mordecai gestured for Frank to pull to the curb.

Frank's jaw dropped. He could not believe what he was seeing.

How in the hell can this be real?

Frank steered his cab to the curb and stopped in front of the old man with the cane. He climbed out of his cab and ran around to the curb. Mordecai was gone, but the old man remained.

"Sir?" Frank's voice was shaking. "Do you need a ride?"

"That would be nice," the man replied, his voice weak with age. "But my check hasn't come in yet. Maybe next time."

"Let's not worry about it this time. Why don't you climb in? I'll help you."

Frank helped the man into the cab and took his place behind the wheel, then he turned his head and spoke over his shoulder. "Where can I take you, sir?"

The old man gave him an address and Frank pulled away

from the curb.

What the hell am I doing?

Frank knew exactly what he was doing. This old man was another opportunity, just like the young woman and child from the other day. Is that why Mordecai had appeared? Was he pointing Frank toward this old man? Frank smiled at the thought.

I think I may actually be losing my mind.

Frank stopped the cab at the address the old man had given to him. He helped the elderly man out of the cab, and was amazed at how the simple gesture made him feel.

Well, if I am going crazy, at least it makes me feel good.

Was Mordecai real, or was he merely hallucinating? He looked forward to his meeting with Sarah and Mike later that night. He had much to share with them.

A few hours later, Frank pulled up in front of the Moon Rock Café. He locked up his cab and went inside.

Sarah spotted Frank as soon as he walked through the door. "Hi, Frank!" She ran over and gave him a brief hug. "Come on. Mike may not be able to make it, but we can still talk." She led him to a booth and offered to get him something to drink.

"No, thank you," Frank replied. He was anxious to share what he had experienced.

Sarah plopped down in the booth across from him. "So, what's new? You look like you have a lot on your mind."

Frank nodded. "I guess I do. You'll never guess what happened to me today."

"You're probably right. Why don't you tell me."

"I saw Mordecai today. He was just standing there on the street corner looking at me. He motioned me over to the curb."

"Oh my God. What did you do?"

"Before I knew it, I was pulling over to the curb. He was standing beside an old man with a cane. When I got there,

I jumped out of the cab and ran around to where they were standing. When I got there, Mordecai was gone."

"What did you do after that?"

"I offered to take the old man wherever he wanted to go. Just like the young woman from the other day, he declined because he had no money."

"And you gave him a ride for free, didn't you?" Sarah was smiling.

"I did. It's the strangest thing. I didn't even question it at the time. I just pulled over, picked up the old man, and took him where he needed to go. It was like Mordecai was directing me to the old man. I know that sounds crazy."

"Maybe to someone else it would, but not to me," Sarah said reassuringly. "What do you think all of this means?"

"I think we're supposed to help people. Plain and simple. I have no idea why we're having these nightmares, or why the man from our dreams is now appearing to me in broad daylight, but it seems obvious to me. He guided me to that old man. The old man needed help and I helped him."

Sarah decided to share her experience too. "I saw him on my way to the subway. Yesterday, in the underground. He was standing there, plain as day, looking right at me. Then, he was just gone."

"It makes me feel better knowing I'm not the only one seeing things."

"I understand. A part of me knows that none of what we are saying is possible, but we can't deny that it is really happening."

"Have you spoken to Mike about what you saw?" Frank asked.

"I have, and you're not going to believe what he told me happened the other day."

Sarah told Frank about George, the construction worker, visiting Mike at the precinct. She told Frank how George was experiencing the same dream, and how he had decided he needed to turn his life around by helping others. She also shared what George said about the accident being his fault.

"There seems to be a common thread here with all of us. Besides the dream haunting our nights, we're all making changes in our lives. We're all trying to help others. You know, it really helps to know I'm not alone in all of this."

"I feel the same way," Sarah said. "I don't know what I would do if I didn't have someone to talk to about it."

Frank smiled. "I should be going. It's been a long day." He slid out of the booth. "Maybe we can still get together with Mike sometime."

"We will. You can count on it."

CHAPTER 35

Sarah stood in the ladies' bathroom at the Moon Rock Café, staring into the mirror. Staring back at her was a woman whose face revealed the fatigue she felt down in her bones. Still, there was a glint of hope in her eyes. She had just finished a conversation with Frank that filled her with both fear and wonder.

Frank was a genuinely kind man and Sarah did not for a second doubt any part of his story. She had a feeling that, somehow, God played a role in everything that was happening. She could not explain why, but she felt that hope was on the horizon.

She heard the door chime. She splashed water on her face and dried it quickly with a handful of paper towels. She rushed out of the bathroom, hoping to find Mike waiting. She was not disappointed.

The café was nearly empty of customers and Sarah was glad. She was ready to talk. Mike sat at his usual spot and Sarah joined him.

"You want something to drink? she asked.

"Not right now, but thanks. Sorry I did not make it here sooner, but something came up."

"That's okay. You just missed Frank. He had some interesting things to say."

"Yeah? We'll have to set up another meet soon. Speaking of interesting things, I dug up a few today that will blow your mind."

"I'm all ears," Sarah replied.

"This afternoon, I was sitting in my car in front of the precinct. I reached up to adjust my rearview mirror and I saw Mordecai in the back seat."

"What?" Sarah gasped.

"Yeah, that was pretty much my reaction. I turned around and he was gone." Mike snapped his fingers. "Just like that."

"You were right. You have definitely had an interesting day."

"Oh, that was just the beginning. There's more. I know who Mordecai is."

Sarah was speechless. She could only try and mouth the words, but could not form them. Finally, she whispered, "How?"

"After getting the hell scared out of me in the car, I went up to my desk. I decided I would look at everything like a cop. I looked at the facts and tried to find connections. I searched for the name 'Mordecai' and got three hits. Two of them didn't pan out, but the last one did. Big time. His name was Mordecai Thomas." Mike told Sarah about finding the file in the archives. He told of the police report and the mugshot that left no doubt that he had found the right man. "He had several run-ins with the law over the years, though it appeared he had cleaned up his act a little the last two years before he died."

"How did he die?" Sarah asked.

"Here's where things get even more interesting. He died one night after accidentally killing a teenager on the Brooklyn Bridge. He had been drinking and was driving home when he struck and killed a teenage girl. The police report stated that he was seen holding the girls' body and sobbing. When the police arrived, he was scared and jumped over the railing, trying to hide. He lost his footing and fell into the river. He was only thirty-eight years old."

"Mike, this changes everything. If Mordecai was a real person, what does that mean? Why is he haunting our dreams, and now our waking hours as well?"

"I've been thinking about that. I'm not really sure, but maybe he's trying to help us. Maybe by helping us, he is somehow helping himself. I know that sounds weird."

"No, not really. It's the best explanation I've heard yet."

"So, you said Frank had some interesting things to say?"

"Yes, he did. The good news is that you and I aren't the only ones who have seen Mordecai outside of our dreams."

Sarah told Mike about Frank's experience. How he had seen Mordecai standing on the corner, the elderly man he helped and his theory that Mordecai was somehow guiding him to people that needed help.

When Sarah had finished, Mike sat in silence. She could see he was being a cop and making the connections.

"You know what?" Mike said, breaking his silence. "I think Frank is onto something."

CHAPTER 36

Frank sat behind the wheel of his cab, trying to calm himself down. He had just made his third trip to Brooklyn, making good on the assignment his boss had given him weeks ago. When he was approaching the bridge he almost turned around, but forced himself to keep going. He had made it safely across the bridge once again and was now waiting outside the building of the law firm called JONES, BUCHANAN & WILLIAMS.

The attractive young woman with long dark hair approached his cab.

"Hi, I'm Beth, thanks for the ride."

She climbed into the back seat and was talking on her cell phone. Frank glanced at her in the rearview mirror and could not believe his eyes. He snapped his head around and looked at her. Fortunately, she was too distracted with her phone call to notice Frank's odd behavior.

She gave him an address in Manhattan, and continued her phone conversation.

What are the odds? This is the woman from my dream, I'm sure of it.

Once again, Frank drove white-knuckled across the Brooklyn Bridge. He breathed a sigh of relief when they had reached Manhattan.

"Sir?" Beth spoke from the back seat. "Do you know of a place where I could get a little something to eat and a good cup of coffee?"

Without thinking, Frank said the first thing that popped into his mind. "The Moon Rock Café is very good."

"Would you mind taking me there? I'll pay extra for the detour of course."

A few minutes later, Frank pulled up in front of the Moon Rock Café. The site of the café, and the memory of his conversation with Sarah, brought a smile to his face.

Beth opened the back door of the cab and climbed out. Leaning back in, she said, "I'll only be about fifteen minutes. Do you mind waiting?"

"I don't mind at all. I'll be right here when you're ready."

Frank watched as Beth entered the café. He had managed to keep his outward composure, but inside he was barely holding it together. Beth was the woman from his dream, he was sure of it. Could the dream be unfolding in real life? What could he do to make it stop?

Frank, just keep it together. Don't start freaking out now.

Frank fought the urge to run inside the café, find Sarah, and tell her what was going on. He wanted to tell her about Beth, and that his dream was becoming real. He was supposed to go to Brooklyn every Tuesday and pick Beth up, and bring her to Manhattan. How was he going to do that? Each time he crossed that bridge, he'd be wondering if it was his last. He rested both hands on the steering wheel, closed his eyes, and took a deep breath. He needed to calm down.

The longer Frank waited, the more anxious he became. He wanted to drive away and not look back. He convinced himself he could stop it all from happening if he just drove away.

To hell with it. I'm out of here.

He started the cab and put it in gear. He checked his rear-view mirror for oncoming traffic, and found himself looking into the eyes of Mordecai.

"Please stay," Mordecai said.

Frank jerked his head around only to find the back seat was empty.

CHAPTER 37

Beth walked into Moon Rock and found an empty table. She was on her way to a meeting and needed a few minutes to gather her thoughts. The ride to Manhattan had left her uneasy. The cab driver looked so familiar, but she knew she had never met him. She shrugged off the feeling until they had arrived at the café. When she had placed her hand on the door handle of the cab, it all came back to her. For a moment, she was transported back to her dream, trapped in the cab on the bridge, with cries for help ringing in her ears. She had almost panicked, but managed to hold it back.

How can this be? Is the dream actually becoming a reality?

She sat at the table, her heart racing, until a waitress placed a glass of ice water on the table. "Hi, my name is Sarah. What can I get you?"

"Coffee please?" Beth asked, her voice shaking.

Sarah returned with the coffee. "Be careful, it's very hot."

"Th-thank you," Beth replied.

"Forgive me, I don't mean to intrude, but you seem to be upset. Is everything okay?" Sarah asked softly.

Beth watched the steam rise from her cup of coffee. "I don't know. I really don't."

Sarah pulled out a chair and sat down. "You can talk to me

if you want. It might help."

Beth looked up from her coffee. "You're probably right, but you will likely think I am crazy."

Sarah smiled. "Oh, you might be surprised. I hear some pretty unusual stories, and even have a few of my own."

Beth did not know why, but Sarah made her feel at ease. She decided talking to her was worth a shot. She offered her hand and said, "My name is Beth."

"Nice to meet you, Beth. Like I said, my name is Sarah. Now, what's on your mind today?"

"Okay. I'm an attorney from Brooklyn. I have an appointment with a client today. I took a cab from my office to Manhattan, which is something I do not typically do. The cab driver who picked me up is the same person who has been in a dream that I've had every night for weeks. In the dream there is an accident on the Brooklyn Bridge. It is a huge car pileup and I am trapped in the back seat of the cab. That cab right there." Beth pointed toward the front door.

Sarah spotted the cab parked in front of the café, turning white as a sheet as the blood drained from her face. "Oh my God," she whispered, barely audible.

Beth reached across the table laid her hand on Sarah's. "Are you okay? Did I say something wrong?"

Sarah squeezed Beth's hand. "No, not at all. Would you excuse me for just a minute? I'll be right back. I promise."

*****

Beth nodded and Sarah made a beeline for the door. She paused on the sidewalk, and leaned over to get a look at the cab driver. It was Frank.

Why am I not surprised?

Frank waved, then got out of the cab and walked over to

where Sarah was standing. "Hi, Sarah. How are you today?" he asked with a nervous smile.

"To tell the truth, I'm not sure, Frank. Did you happen to drop off a woman with long brown hair? She said she's an attorney."

Frank's smile vanished. "Yes. Why do you ask?"

"She's sitting in there at a table. I could see she was upset about something and we got to talking. She had a very interesting story about a dream she's been having every night for weeks. She's in an accident, on the Brooklyn Bridge and trapped in a cab. Your cab."

"I knew it. As soon as she got in my cab, I knew it was her."

"Can you wait a while longer?" Sarah asked. "I need to talk to her some more. Maybe she has some pieces of the puzzle that will help us all figure this out. Do you mind?"

"No, of course I don't mind. We have to figure this out. I'll wait all day if I have to."

Sarah gave Frank a quick hug. "Say a little prayer for me. I'm going back inside."

CHAPTER 38

Sarah entered the café and made her way to the ladies'
bathroom. She checked her appearance in the mirror as she
braced herself for the conversation she was about to continue
with Beth.

If she only knew. She was about to find out.

Sarah left the bathroom and rejoined Beth at her table.

"Is everything okay?" Beth asked. "I'm sorry I dumped all
of that on you. You must think I'm out of my mind."

"I don't think that at all. Tell me more about the dreams
you've been having. You said you were stuck in the cab after
an accident. What happened next?" Sarah was fairly certain
she knew the answer.

Beth laid it all out for Sarah. She told her about the accident: the fumes and the cries for help, a man in black approaching her.

Sarah leaned in closer. "Did the man tell you his name or
say anything?"

"Okay, this is going to sound weird. He didn't tell me his
name, but I know it's Mordecai. Don't ask me how I know, I
just do. He does talk to me though. He tells me everything will
be okay, and I think he's trying to open the door of the cab.
Am I going crazy?"

Sarah smiled and tried to sound as reassuring as possible. "No, you don't sound crazy. I promise."

"I just want the dreams to stop, you know? I'm not sleeping, I'm exhausted every day, and I feel like my whole world has been turned upside down."

Sarah nodded. "Believe me, I know what that feels like."

"I suppose there has been some good that has come from all of this. It has caused me take a hard look at my life. I was inspired to become a lawyer by my uncle Henry. He was my mentor, and my example of what it meant to live a life dedicated to helping others. He was killed a few years ago, and since that day I've grown increasingly bitter. I guess I lost my way and forgot who I was, and who I wanted to be. I've been too wrapped up in myself to see what I have become. I decided I'm through living that way, and no matter what happens with these dreams, I will honor my uncle's legacy. In fact, that's the reason for my trip to Manhattan today. I'm doing some pro bono work for a single mother."

Sarah smiled. "Beth, I'm about to share something with you that will either make you feel better, or convince you that we're both crazy."

Beth raised an eyebrow at Sarah. "Okay, fire away."

Sarah started at the beginning. She told Beth her version of the dream, and that there were at least three others who were having the same dream. "One of those people happens to be your cab driver out there." Sarah nodded toward the street. "His name is Frank and we only recently met."

Beth's eyes grew wide as Sarah continued her story. "How is this possible and what does it mean?"

"That's the question isn't it? We're all wondering the same thing, but we're also coming up with a similar response. Each one of us has begun reevaluating our lives, and not liking what we see. We now all seem drawn to something outside of ourselves and have a desire to help others in some way." Sarah looked outside at Frank's cab. "Take Frank out there for example. He believes that Mordecai is somehow guiding him to people that are in need of help."

CHAPTER 39

Frank waited patiently, more or less, in his cab. It had been longer than fifteen minutes, but he didn't care. He would wait all day if he had to, he just wanted some answers.

He was shocked when Sarah had walked out of the café to talk to him. Beth had only been inside for a few minutes. Sarah had apparently wasted no time connecting with the woman.

Frank marveled at how all of this had come about. First the dreams, and then the sequence of events that led him over the bridge into Brooklyn to pick up the very woman who had been inhabiting his nightmares. It was surreal. He had seen the way the woman had looked at him, and was sure she had recognized him as well. Based on what Sarah had told him, he was sure of it. His anxiety level began to increase, and he once again considered driving away. He remembered what happened the last time though, so he decided to stay put. He avoided looking into the rearview mirror.

Frank noticed Beth and Sarah walking out of the café. He had rolled the windows down and could hear their conversation.

"I don't come to Manhattan often," Beth said, "but I would love to talk with you again. The sooner the better."

"I would like that very much. Thank you for sharing your

story. I know how difficult it was for you. This is all connected somehow. We'll figure it out together," Sarah replied. "Can we exchange phone numbers so we can stay in touch?"

"Absolutely!" Beth said, handing Sarah a business card.

Sarah pulled a pen and piece of paper from her apron. She jotted down her number and handed it to Beth. The two women hugged one another.

Frank watched as Sarah ducked back inside the café, and Beth turned back toward the cab. His heart was pounding.

CHAPTER 40

Beth plopped down in the back seat and closed the door. "Thanks for waiting, Frank."

Frank did not remember telling her his name. Sarah must have told her everything. He turned to face her. "I guess Sarah told you my name?"

"She did, and a lot more besides." Beth smiled. "I know about the dreams you've been having, and I've been having them too. Apparently, so has Sarah and a couple of other people. I had a great conversation with Sarah about all of this. She said that your theory was that Mordecai was guiding you to people in need. Is that right?"

Frank swallowed, wondering where to begin. "Yeah, I suppose I do feel that way. It's happened a couple of times." He told Beth about the young woman and baby he had helped. He told her about his epiphany he experienced after dropping them off. He barely knew Beth, but he found himself telling her everything. He even told her about seeing Mordecai, and how he had been directed to the old man with the cane.

"Frank, that is amazing. It sounds like you've been going through a kind of transformation." Beth glanced at her watch. "Oh my gosh! I'm going to be late. Do you mind if we leave now? I'll talk while you drive."

Frank put the cab in gear and, with some hesitation, glanced at the rearview mirror. The way was clear and Mordecai was not there. Relieved, he pulled away from the curb and into the street.

Once they were under way, Beth continued, "I can relate to much of what you've said, Frank. The dreams have me walking a fine line between sanity and going completely nuts, but they've also been the catalyst which has caused me to take a hard look at my life. Needless to say, I wasn't too happy with what I saw. I was inspired to be a lawyer by my uncle Henry. He was a great man, and lived his life helping people who had nowhere else to turn. I wanted to be like him. He was killed, and after that I lost my way. I realize that now, and I am making a change. In fact, I am on my way today to take up my first pro bono case."

Frank glanced at Beth in the rearview mirror. "I think the more I step outside of my own life and extend kindness to someone else, the happier I will be. I don't know if it will help make these dreams stop, but at least my days will be bearable." He was fighting back his emotions.

Beth changed the subject. "How long have you known Sarah?

"Not long at all. I met her just a few days ago. Long story, but I ended up in the café and overheard her talking with someone about the dreams she was having. I heard enough to know that she was having dreams much like mine. I went back a couple of days later and talked with her about it."

"Sarah is certainly easy to talk to. I'm glad I met her today … and you."

"Me too," Frank replied sheepishly.

*****

Beth and Frank arrived at the address she had given him, and he pulled to the curb. Beth dug in her purse, looking for her billfold.

Frank turned to face Beth. "It's on me today."

Beth looked up and started to protest. She saw the look in Frank's eyes and knew it would do no good. She smiled warmly. "Thank you, Frank. I appreciate you."

Frank looked away, embarrassed. "Maybe we can get together with Sarah soon and talk about this some more."

"Yes, let's plan on it. Have a great day!" Beth climbed out of the cab and disappeared into the crowd.

CHAPTER 41

George gathered together his stash of reusable doors and windows. He loaded them all into the back of his truck and tied them down. He pulled a piece of paper from his pocket, on which he had written the number for Habitat for Humanity. He remembered how he felt the day he first noticed the billboard. It felt as though he had received a sign from heaven, and just maybe he had.

He slammed shut the tailgate of his truck, and caught a glimpse of the faded tattoo on his forearm. He had gotten it years ago when he was a teenager involved with the youth group of his church. The tattoo read, "Isaiah 6:8," but George still remembered the entire verse by heart: "Then I heard the voice of the Lord saying, 'Whom shall I send? And who will go for us?' And I said, 'Here am I. Send me!'"

George remembered how much that verse had meant to his mother. She used to tell him that everyone was chosen, but few answered the call. She cautioned him to always be listening.

I'm listening now, Mom.

He climbed into his truck and dialed the number on the piece of paper. He waited while the phone rang, his eyes filling with tears. It may not be much, but he would do what he could. He only wished his mom was still alive. She would be so proud of him.

He talked to the people at Habitat for Humanity and let them know he was on the way with a donation. The nightmares would take a back seat today. He had more important things to do.

When he arrived at the Habitat for Humanity distribution and receiving center, he got out of his truck and went inside. He told the young woman at the front desk who he was and why he was there. She thanked him and asked him to pull around the building to the unloading docks. There was a crew waiting to help him unload.

George was smiling as he climbed back into his truck. He felt better than he had in a long time. He backed his truck up to the dock and climbed out. He was greeted by a happy crew of young men wearing work gloves. They all pitched in and began unloading the truck, George working with them side by side.

When they had finished, George walked up to one of the young men and handed him a piece of paper with his name and phone number written on it. "When you guys get ready to start your next project, please give me a call. I would love to help."

The young man accepted his offer and they shook hands.

George pulled out of the parking lot, and back onto the highway. As he drove, he glanced up at the blue sky above.

Thanks, Mom.

CHAPTER 42

Sarah was busy working when she heard the café door chime. She turned and saw that it was Mike. He was wearing a broad smile, something she had not seen on him for a long time. He walked to his booth, which was somehow available. It was uncanny how that always seemed to be the case when he arrived.

It had been a few days since they had seen each other and both were eager to catch up. Sarah, as usual, met Mike at his table with a cup of coffee.

Mike was the first to speak. "I'm kind of excited about something, but I want to hear what you have been up to since we last met."

Sarah slowly exhaled and sat down. "Wow. Where to begin?"

Mike chuckled. "The beginning?"

"Well, I've kind of started a new thing. Every day, the café has leftover pastries and food that wasn't sold that day. I talked to Liz and we came up with a plan. Instead of tossing out, and wasting, all of that food, I'm going to take it to a local soup kitchen called the Potter's Plate."

"That sounds great!"

"It is, and I took my first batch there yesterday. You should have seen them, Mike. They were so excited about it and asked if I'd like to stay and help serve. I called my babysitter and arranged for her to stay with the girls for a couple more hours while I stayed at the soup kitchen. It was the greatest experience. You know, I have been waiting tables for a long time, but it never felt as good as serving those people last night. There were no complaints and everyone seemed so grateful to have something to eat. It reminded me of a Bible verse I learned when I was a little girl. It's from Isaiah if I remember correctly. It says, 'But those who wait on the Lord, shall renew their strength, they shall mount up on wings like eagles, they shall run and not be weary, they shall walk and not be faint.' I can't believe I still remember that."

Mike grinned. "Since when do you go around quoting Bible verses?"

"I know, right? But it just popped into my mind last night while I was helping out at the soup kitchen. Seeing all of those people, who literally have nothing, smile at the site of a plate of food filled my heart with joy and peace. I can't explain it. For a few hours I didn't have one thought about our crazy dreams."

"It's good to see you so happy. It's been a while."

"Look who's talking," Sarah teased. "You walked in here today with a huge smile on your face. What are you so excited about?"

"Well, you know how we've been talking about trying to make a difference? I thought of something I could do and asked my captain about it. He gave me the thumbs-up and I have to admit, I'm pretty stoked."

"What was your idea?"

"I had the idea to start a mentoring program for troubled youth in our neighborhood. It would give them a chance to get off the streets and maybe learn a better way to live. We're going to name the program after my father." Mike was beaming.

"That is such great news! I am so proud of you, Mike."

"Thanks. I feel pretty good about it. Like you, it made me forget about the nightmares, at least for a while."

More people were spilling into the café. It looked like Sarah would have to get back to work.

Mike noticed the crowd. "Looks like you're about to get busy."

Sarah nodded. "Yes, I need to get back to work. I have so much more to tell you. Remember Frank, the cab driver? He was here today. He dropped off a lady who you will want to meet."

"What lady? Why would I want to meet her?"

"Her name is Beth, she's a lawyer from Brooklyn. She's having the dreams too. Look, I have to get back to work. Can you come by again tomorrow so we can talk?"

"Yes, I can do that."

"Great. I'll see you then." Sarah slid out of the booth and rushed away.

CHAPTER 43

Beth sat at her desk, separating a mound of files into two separate stacks. The stack on her right was already ten high, the one on her left only five. The tallest stack of files were cases she was considering to do pro bono, while the other stack were paying clients. She found it mildly amusing that the majority of the work she was planning would not make her any money whatsoever. She would be okay though, thanks to her uncle Henry. In his will, he had provided a substantial trust fund for Beth. She had barely touched it over the years, being determined to prove to the world that she could make her own way. She no longer cared about what the world thought of her. She knew that her uncle had hopes that she would follow in his footsteps, providing help to those who had no one else they could depend on. The trust fund was his way to ensure she would have all that she needed. She was determined to honor his wishes.

Beth stood up from her desk, stretching her tired muscles. She walked over and looked through her office window at the beautiful sunset.

Thank you, God, for giving me Uncle Henry.

She remembered the story her uncle had told her of how he first became interested in becoming a lawyer. He told her he was sitting in church one day and heard the preacher quote a verse from the book of Psalms.

"Your righteousness is everlasting, and your law is true."

Beth knew it was from Psalm 119:142 because it used to hang on a plaque in her uncle's office. His zest for life had been contagious, and she missed him deeply. She took solace in knowing he would be proud of her now.

CHAPTER 44

Sarah awoke to the familiar smell of gasoline and smoke. She heard the familiar voices crying out for help. In the midst of it all was Mordecai, calling her name and telling her it was okay.

It's not okay.

Mordecai's voice had been so clear that she looked all around her room to make sure she was alone. Sarah could not wait to get to work, and to leave her nightmares behind. Tori, her babysitter, had been nice enough to drop by and take her girls to school. The apartment was quiet and the silence was getting to her. She needed to be busy.

Sarah walked the familiar route to the subway. She then descended the steps and entered the underground, along with a few hundred other people. As she waited for her train, she glanced across the tracks to see Mordecai staring back at her from the other side. He eyes widened and just as she was about to call out, a train passed between them. When the train had passed, Mordecai was gone. She looked around at the other commuters to see if anyone else had seen Mordecai. If they had, there was no indication

When Sarah arrived at the Moon Rock, she tied on her

apron quickly and got right to work. After the morning rush, she sat down at a table to rest her feet. The door chimed and in walked Mike, along with George and Frank. She had not seen the three of them together since the day of the argument out in the street.

Mike spotted Sarah and motioned for the men to head in her direction. The three men greeted Sarah and sat down.

Sarah was not sure why, but she was nervous. There was something about all of them being together that made her feel uneasy. "What brings you three here today?"

"Fair question," Mike said. "Believe it or not, it wasn't planned. I ran into George at the gas station down the street. We talked for a minute and decided we'd come here and see if you had a few minutes to talk. When we got here, Frank was just parking out front. Kind of weird, huh?"

"Yeah, you could say that," Sarah replied, her tone indicating she thought it was way beyond weird.

"No doubt," Mike agreed. "George and I were talking about how we have all been going through changes of one kind or another. Based on what Frank told you the other day, George has been going through similar changes. I've been thinking that, maybe, that's what this is all about. What do you guys think?"

Everyone agreed and Mike continued, "Whatever happens, or doesn't happen, on the Brooklyn Bridge is out of our control. What we can control is the present moment, and how we live our lives each day. We may never know why we are all having these dreams, or why Mordecai appears in them, but I have to believe we still have a say in how we live."

"Will you excuse me for a minute?" Sarah abruptly stood up and walked to the ladies' bathroom.

George and Frank both looked at Mike.

"I don't know what that was about. You guys hang out here,

I'll be back." Mike got up and walked toward the bathrooms. He waited outside the door for Sarah to come out.

Finally, after a few minutes, Sarah came out of the bathroom. Her eyes were red and Mike could see she had been crying.

"Sarah, what's wrong?"

"I don't know. All of us being here together, it's just a little overwhelming."

Mike reached out and squeezed Sarah's shoulder. "Damn, I'm sorry. I shouldn't have surprised you like that."

"You don't have to apologize. You didn't do anything wrong. It's just a lot to take in. It's different for me talking one on one, but now that there's five of—"

"Five?" Mike interrupted. "You mean four."

"I keep forgetting you haven't met Beth. Remember I told you that Frank brought a woman here to the café? A lawyer from Brooklyn? Well, she's been having the same dreams. So that makes five of us."

Mike stepped over and wrapped his arms around Sarah.

Sarah buried her face into Mike's chest, fighting back tears. After a moment, she pulled back. "I'm okay, Mike. Thank you."

Mike brushed Sarah's hair back from her face. "Are you sure? We don't have to talk right now if you're not up to it."

"I'm good, seriously. I want to talk."

"Okay. Let's head back and see if George and Frank are still here. They might have spooked and left too." Mike grinned.

Sarah punched him teasingly, and they walked back to their table. George and Frank were still there, plus one more person. They had been joined by Beth.

Sarah was surprised. "Beth? When did you get here?"

"I walked in a few minutes ago. I saw Frank and came over to see if he wanted to finish our chat."

"I assume you've been introduced to George," and I'm

Mike, he surmised.

"I have, thank you," Beth replied. "I understand that the five of us share a common bond."

"Indeed, we do," Mike agreed.

They all took a seat at the table. Sarah glanced at Frank, and then George. "Sorry about that guys. This is all a bit overwhelming sometimes," she explained.

"It's okay, Sarah," Frank said. "I think we all feel the same way."

George nodded. "I know I do."

"Certainly goes for me too," Beth chimed in.

Mike pulled out a file folder and laid it gently on the table. "I've been thinking a lot about Mordecai. Maybe if we understand more about who he was, it can help us figure out why he is appearing to us in our dreams, or for some of us, even while we're awake."

Frank was about to speak, but George spoke first. "What do you mean find out more about who he was? Are you saying he was a real person?"

Mike nodded. "That's exactly what I'm saying. I did some digging and I found this old file in the archives room down at my precinct." Mike pulled out the old mugshot and laid it on top of the file folder. "This guy look familiar to everyone?"

They all stared at the photograph and could not believe their eyes. Frank picked up the picture for a closer look. When he finished, he passed it to Beth. While everyone was passing around the picture, Mike read to them from the police report.

Mike finished reading and closed the file. "Like I was saying, maybe by understanding who he was, and how he died, it will help us figure this out. Maybe Mordecai is seeking forgiveness, or looking to make up for what he did by helping us. Am I out in left field on this?"

CHAPTER 45

Sarah had gotten coffee and pastries for everyone at the table. They sipped coffee and snacked on the pastries as they discussed Mike's theory.

Frank spoke up before anyone else. "I don't think you're coming from left field at all, Mike. The entire situation seems impossible, not to mention crazy, but it is happening nevertheless. And it is happening to all five of us. Like all of you, I'd love nothing more than for these nightmares to stop, but the most important thing is the changes that we are making in our lives."

"I couldn't agree more." George said. "I finally feel like I'm the man my mother prayed that I would become. I wouldn't trade that feeling for anything. Not even for these nightmares to end."

"I second that," Beth said. "I feel the same about my uncle Henry. Isn't this amazing? Look at us. A cab driver, policeman, construction worker, waitress, and a lawyer. We couldn't be more different, yet here we are together. We come from different walks of life, and maybe that's the point."

"So we can affect change in the lives of many different people." Sarah shared Beth's vision.

George nodded enthusiastically. "Yeah, if we can focus on

the good we can do instead of our nightmares, maybe that's how we can eventually rid ourselves of them."

"Maybe the dreams are just a wake-up call," Mike said. "One that we apparently needed."

CHAPTER 46

The midmorning slump was over and the café began to get busy again. Sarah stood up from the table. "Okay, you guys. I've got to get back to work."

Sarah hugged each person as they all said their good-byes. Everyone made sure they had exchanged phone numbers.

Mike hung back as Sarah cleared off the table. "I think that went pretty well, do you?"

"Yes, I think so too."

Mike touched Sarah's arm. "Are you doing okay? I know this was a lot."

"I'm fine, Mike, really. It was good that we all finally got together."

"Agreed," Mike said. "I think we will eventually get this figured out."

"I think so too, and I agree with what you said earlier about the dreams being a wake-up call. Since I have made a conscious effort to change, and have begun helping others instead of feeling sorry for myself, I feel like a new person. My experience at the Potter's Plate just reinforced that for me. If I could wish for anything other than that right now, it would be a good night's sleep." Sarah smiled weakly.

"Same here. I'm sure the others would agree. I'm going to run. Talk to you soon."

"Be safe, Mike. Talk to you soon."

CHAPTER 47

Sarah and Liz closed down the Moon Rock, and Sarah headed for the subway. Even though she looked forward to seeing her daughters, she was in no hurry to relive the dream she knew would come. She had made big changes in her life lately, but the dreams gave her no respite. Making matters worse was the fact that the dreams were becoming more realistic each night.

She paused outside her apartment door, fumbling with her keys. She slid the key in the lock and opened the door. Rose and Emma heard the door and came running to meet her.

"Hi girls, how are you?" Sarah said. Her spirits were always lifted when she saw her kids.

Tori came in from the kitchen. "Hi, Sarah!"

"Hi, Tori. Sorry I'm running a bit late."

"No worries, Miss Sarah." Tori gathered up the puzzles on the floor. When she finished, she grabbed her backpack and hugged the girls good night. "I'll see you girls in the morning. Bright and early!"

"Tori, I don't know where you get your energy, but thanks!" Sarah said, taking down her ponytail. She locked the door and turned to face her daughters. "You girls ready for a bedtime story?

The girls shouted with glee and ran off to their room, with Sarah on the heels. She tucked them both in bed, kissed them, and grabbed the book she had been reading to them. It was called *The Giving Tree* and it was one of their favorites. By the time Sarah had finished the book, both girls were nearly asleep.

"Sweet dreams, girls. Mommy loves you." Sarah whispered, dimming the lights.

"We love you, Mommy," they answered in unison.

Sarah thought about the book she had just read to her daughters. She found it a bit ironic that, considering recent events, one of their favorite books was about giving and caring for others.

Sarah got herself ready for bed, though she wondered if it was worth the effort. She knew the dream awaited her return and that rest would not come. She slipped under the covers, then pulled them up to her chest. Soon, she slipped into a deep slumber and back into the dream.

The smoke and fumes made it hard to breathe. She could feel the glass in her face and the pain coming from her shoulder. Mordecai was there, calling to her.

"Sarah, let me help you. Take my hand."

Then the dream took a different turn. Sarah closed her eyes, and trusting Mordecai's words, extended her hand. She felt his strong grasp and the next thing she knew she was standing next to Mordecai outside of the bus. Mordecai touched her face and then her shoulder. The pain in both slowly subsided. She felt confused and disoriented. Without another word, they began walking away from the bus and through the thick fog.

Suddenly, she was standing in front of Mike's patrol car. She looked through the cracked windshield and directly into Mike's eyes.

"Sarah? Is that you?"

Sarah's jaw dropped. He could see her!

Sarah awoke with a start, her heart beating hard in her chest.

"Oh my God."

She could not believe what happened. She had not only surrendered to Mordecai, and allowed him to remove her from the wreckage, but she saw Mike and he had seen her.

This can't be happening. It was just part of the dream.

Her phone on the night stand buzzed, indicating she had received a text message. She glanced at the clock: 6 a.m.

Who on earth could this be?

She grabbed her phone and swiped the screen. It was Mike. Mike hated text messaging and seldom, if ever, texted anyone. She read his text.

"Are you okay?"

Why would he ask me that? Could it be the dream? She could not fathom that as a possibility. She responded to his message. "Yes, why do you ask?"

"Can you meet me at the park in a couple of hours?"

She agreed to meet him and then dragged herself out of bed. Her heart was still pounding, as much from reading Mike's text as from the dream. Something very unusual must have happened for Mike to have texted her and ask for a meeting so soon.

Sarah took a fast shower, got dressed, and walked into the living room. Tori had already let herself in and had the girls all ready for school.

"Tori, you are such a blessing. I don't know what I would do without you."

"No worries, Miss Sarah. I love you and the girls! Besides, the extra money helps me with school." Tori winked, then ushered the girls out the door.

CHAPTER 48

Frank pulled up across the street from the job site where George worked. He could see George in the distance, loading various items into the back of his truck. He blew the horn and waved.

George waved back and walked across the street. He yanked a work glove from his right hand and offered it to his new friend.

Frank accepted and shook it vigorously. "How are you doing, George?"

"I'm doing okay. How 'bout you? What brings you out this way?"

"I figured you would be getting off work about now. I wanted to drop by and see how you were holding up."

George was visibly moved. "Well, I appreciate that, Frank. I really do. I guess I'm doing okay. Tired due to lack of sleep, but I'm guessing you know all about that."

"That I do, my friend. I want you to know I admire what you're doing." Frank gestured toward George's truck.

"I'm just trying to do my part in making a difference in the world. I admire what you're doing too. Like we talked about the other day, I think this may be what it's all about. Just caring enough to help other people."

"I agree. What really matters is that we make the best of the opportunities we have. How about we meet up again at the Moon Rock in a couple of days?"

"I think that's a great idea. Maybe the others can be there too. We might figure this out yet."

"Great! I'll see you then. If you need anything in the meantime, you have my number."

"Ditto," George replied.

George walked back to his truck. Seeing it loaded down with supplies that he knew would directly benefit someone in need did his heart good.

CHAPTER 49

Beth walked her client to the door. It was her third pro bono case so far and she had never felt better. It was the young mother who was seeking help from an uncaring ex-husband. She had been working two jobs and was weary to the bone. The client had been amazed that Beth would represent her free of charge. She had been speechless and the tears flowed. Beth hoped that Uncle Henry was smiling down from heaven.

Even though the nightmares kept coming, she would not stray from the path she now walked. She looked at her reflection in the glass door of her office and imagined she could see Uncle Henry standing with his arm around her. She knew she was on the right path at last.

She walked back toward her desk and sat down. She flipped open another case file, but her thoughts drifted back to the dream from the night before. It had felt so real, and this time things were different. She remembered being trapped in the back of the cab and calling out to Frank.

"Frank! Frank can you help me!" she had cried. Once again, Mordecai arrived and spoke to her. He wanted to help her, but she remembered not wanting to leave Frank behind.

Her desk phone began to ring, snapping her back to reality. As if she could tell the difference anymore.

She let the call go to voicemail and continued reading the file in front of her. It would be her next pro bono project.

CHAPTER 50

Sarah exited the train and headed for the stairs that would take her above ground to the street. The text message she received from Mike earlier that morning had left her shaken. It was more than the fact that Mike seldom, if ever, used text messaging as a form of communication. It was that he texted her immediately after they had seen each other in her dream. Mike had asked her to meet him in Central Park, for what reason she did not know. The suspense caused her to quicken her pace.

She took the stairs two at a time, weaving around the slower paced commuters. One of the people on the other side of the stairway caught her eye. It was a tall man dressed from head to toe in black, and he was staring at her. She did a double take as she passed him.

Mordecai!

A familiar chill ran through her body. She stopped on the stairwell and turned back, but he was gone. She turned and ran the rest of the way up the stairs. She did not slow down when she reached street level, but ran straight into the park. She could see Mike in the distance, already waiting for her on a bench. Not wanting to draw attention to herself, she covered the rest of the distance at a normal pace.

*****

Mike saw Sarah approaching. Her face was flushed and she seemed almost scared.

He stood and placed his hands on her shoulders. "Sarah, what's wrong?"

Sarah was out of breath. "I saw him, Mike. On the stairs leading to the subway. It was him. It was Mordecai."

"Come on. Sit down and catch your breath." Mike sat down and gestured for Sarah to sit beside him. He gave her a few minutes to calm down before speaking. "You okay?" he asked.

"Yes, I'm fine. As good as I can be considering I keep seeing a ghost everywhere I go."

"I'm sorry about texting you so early this morning."

"It's okay. I was just surprised you texted at all. I know that's not your thing."

"True. I almost called, but I was afraid it might wake up your girls."

Sarah took a long, deep breath and slowly exhaled. She was finally calming down from having seen Mordecai. "So, what's going, Mike? Why did you want to meet this morning?"

"I saw you in the dream last night. You saw me too, didn't you?"

"I did. What does that mean?"

Mike leaned forward, elbows on his knees, and his head in his hands. "I'm not sure. You were with Mordecai."

"It was strange. It was different last night. When Mordecai came to the bus, and reached out his hand to help, I took it. He pulled me from the wreckage, and somehow removed the glass from my face. The pain went away too. Next thing I know we are standing in front of your car and I'm looking at you. I heard you speak to me."

"I know. I heard you too. This is getting crazier every day."

Mike leaned back on the bench. "I wonder if the others are experiencing anything different."

"I wondered the same thing. I think they're all kind of looking to us for answers, but I don't know what to tell them."

"Yeah, same here. I think we are just as mystified about all of this as they are. It's good we all have each other though. I know Frank and George are staying in touch with each other."

"That's good. I should probably reach out to Beth too."

"Let me ask you something, Sarah. Last night, in the dream, were you aware that you were dreaming? Like when you saw me, were you aware of what was happening?"

"It seemed so real, Mike, but I'm not sure."

"I think I was aware, but I can't be sure. I'm wondering if there's a way we could will ourselves to not wake up, and see if the dream would play itself out."

Sarah thought for a minute before speaking. "That may be possible. I do know that I purposely did something different last night. When Mordecai comes to the bus offering to help, I typically wake up scared half to death. Last night, I actually decided to take his hand instead. So, you may be onto something. I wasn't as afraid last night. Is that weird?"

"I don't think so, and I feel pretty much the same. I'm not as scared of the dreams either, and the more I think about it, the more I am convinced that Mordecai is trying to help himself as much as us. Maybe by helping us, he somehow helps himself."

Sarah turned sideways on the bench and faced Mike. "Think about what you just said, Mike. It makes sense. All five of us, as a result of having these dreams, have been making significant changes in our lives. We are all finding that, by helping other people, we are helping ourselves. We are all happier and feel like we are making a difference. It makes perfect sense that the same thing would apply to Mordecai."

"You're right. It does make sense. I guess we may be on the right track after all."

Sarah nodded in agreement. "I think that we are."

"I spoke to George recently and told him we should get together again. I asked him to come by the Moon Rock tomorrow, and to bring Frank too. Is that okay?"

"Of course. We need to see if the others have had any different experiences too."

"Sounds good. I better get to work. I will talk to you later. Thank you for meeting with me on such short notice."

Sarah smiled. "Anytime. That's what friends are for."

CHAPTER 51

Frank could see Beth in the back seat of his cab. She was beat up and crying for help. He was trapped as well and felt helpless. Suddenly, Mordecai appeared outside Beth's window. He was trying to help her. Frank was amazed at how calm Mordecai appeared to be, in spite of the circumstances.

Beth was frightened. She looked at Mordecai through the shattered window, and then at Frank. She kept trying the door handle, but the door would not budge.

Frank worked to free himself, but it was no use. His legs were pinned beneath the dashboard. He turned to say something to Beth, and she was gone.

Where is she? Did Mordecai get her out?

Beth was in shock. She was standing next to Mordecai outside of the demolished cab. She did not remember how, but he must have gotten her out. They stood there, fog mixed with smoke swirling around them. Mordecai took Beth's hand and led her around to the other side of the cab. They stopped when they reached the driver's door, and Beth could see Frank struggling to free himself. He was coughing from the fumes, and a trickle of blood ran down his forehead.

Frank heard Mordecai asking him to open the door. He turned and was shocked to see Beth standing outside of his door. She grabbed the outside door handle and yanked the door open. Frank was able to crawl out of the cab, and Beth helped him to his feet.

Mordecai was gone.

Frank leaned back against the hood of the cab, and looked at Beth. In between coughing fits, he managed to speak. "Are you okay?"

Beth nodded and took Frank by the hand. They set out walking across the bridge and into the fog. Both were amazed to be alive.

Beth entered her office like a woman on a mission. The dream last night had been intense, and all too real. It was different than before, because she had actually escaped the wreckage and had even helped Frank. She did not know what to make of it, and wondered if Frank had dreamed it the same way. She stopped by the coffee pot, grabbed a cup of coffee, and headed down the hall toward her office.

The first thing Beth noticed when she reached her desk was a stack of mail left by her assistant. On top of the stack was a hot-pink envelope that was obviously a card. She walked around her desk and sat down. She picked up the envelope and checked the return address. It was from the young mother she had recently helped. It was the first pro bono case she had handled since rediscovering her calling. She had won the case, and the young woman's life had been changed for the better.

Beth opened the envelope and read the card, which included a handwritten message. Tears filled her eyes as she read the heartfelt expression of gratitude.

That was all the payment she would ever need. She had found her calling, just like Uncle Henry had before her.

God, thank you for opening my eyes.

CHAPTER 52

Mike sat at his desk, staring in disbelief at the brand-new manual in front of him. On the front cover, in gilded letters, were the words *Captain Michael Nelson Sr.'s NYPD Mentoring Program.* Mike felt the lump in his throat as he ran his fingers over the gold lettering.

Dad would be proud.

Mike finally felt that he was doing something that would actually make a difference. His life had new meaning, and for that he was grateful. The icing on the cake was that his father's legacy would continue. He could not wait to show Sarah.

Maybe it's been worth it. Maybe the dreams have been leading me to this moment.

He was glad he had met Sarah that morning to talk about the dream. He could not begin to comprehend how they could share the same dream, and even talk to one another. It was mind-boggling to say the least. Mordecai had helped Sarah escape the bus, which proved the theory Mike had been working on. That Mordecai was there to help, not harm, and was likely helping himself in the process.

Sarah wasn't the only one Mordecai helped in the previous night's dream. Mike remembered Mordecai opening the door of his police car, and dragging him free of the wreckage. He had walked, side by side, with Mordecai into the fog.

They came upon Frank and Beth and they were all so happy to find one another. Then, Mordecai was simply gone.

Mike found himself feeling sorry for Mordecai. The man had died a tragic death, after having just begun to turn his life around. Mike believed that God had allowed Mordecai to return and to help him and his new friends have an opportunity at a new life.

Mike was determined to make the most of his opportunity.

CHAPTER 53

Frank parked his cab in front of the Moon Rock. He had come to love the café, and the new friends he had made there. His mind was still consumed with the dream he had the night before. It felt so real, and this time it was different. He and Beth had both escaped the wreckage, and had even found Mike in the fog. Mordecai, as usual, had vanished.

Frank realized that for the first time since the dreams began, he did not record it in the notepad by his bed.

It doesn't matter. I don't need to keep count anymore.

Frank was happier than he had been in years. Yes, he wished the dreams would stop, but the way he lived his days now made it all worthwhile. The looks on people's faces when he told them, "This one's on me," was all the payment he would ever need. He also had four new friends who understood, and who had also changed.

Frank climbed out of his cab and went inside. He spotted Sarah behind the counter, and walked over to a stool. He sat down and said, "Hi, Sarah! It's good to see you today."

"Hello, Frank! How are you?"

"I'm doing well, I really am. Can I get a quick cup of coffee?"

"Absolutely." Sarah smiled and grabbed a mug.

Frank leaned over the counter and whispered, "The dream was different for me last night. Was it for you?"

"Yes, it was. Mordecai helped me out of the wreckage."

Frank sipped his coffee, then wiped his mouth with the back of his hand. "Same here. He helped Beth and Mike too. This is unbelievable."

"I know what you mean. In the end, I think Mike was right. I think Mordecai has been trying to help us, and maybe himself at the same time."

"I know all of us have changed, and changed for the better. So I suppose I agree with you. I think Mordecai, in his own way, is searching for peace. I pray he finds it."

"Me too, Frank. I wish the dreams would stop, but I'm grateful for how all of our lives have changed. It hasn't been easy, but I think it's been worth it. I feel like I have to make up for lost time."

"I know what you mean, but there's no use worrying about the past. I think that taking it one day at a time is the key."

"You're right. Fighting the good fight, but one day at a time."

Frank laid money on the counter. "Well said. I'm off to work. Talk to you later?"

Sarah grinned. "Count on it."

CHAPTER 54

George sat motionless in a chair inside a tattoo shop. The artist was hard at work putting fresh ink on George's faded Isaiah 6:8 tattoo.

George got his first tattoo when he was only seventeen. The verse had meant a lot to him, and the tattoo was a way of reminding him that if the world was to be changed, it was up to him to do his part. Later, as the years passed, the tattoo faded along with his belief.

When the artist had finished, George looked at the tattoo approvingly. He paid and walked out of the shop to his truck. It felt good to have the tattoo freshened up, and he felt that the same had happened to his faith. He reached his truck and unlocked the door with his remote. A flyer stapled to a telephone pole by his truck caught his eye. It was an ad promoting Habitat for Humanity. He smiled and took the flyer as confirmation that he was on the right track.

George had come to accept that the nightmares had been a wake-up call, not only for him, but for his four new friends as well. He wanted the dreams to stop, but knew it had been worth it.

George sat in his truck and replayed in his mind the dream he had the night before.

He had been thrown from his truck, and lay injured on the ledge of the bridge. Mordecai had arrived, as usual, and offered George his hand. What was different about last night's dream was that this time, George accepted. The next thing he remembered was walking away with Mordecai and into the fog. He no longer felt pain from his injuries.

George stuck his key in the ignition and started the engine. He pulled away from the curb and headed toward Manhattan. His thoughts drifted to memories of his mother. She had been the strongest person George ever knew. When she encountered trials in life, her faith just grew that much stronger. She made a habit of telling George that when life got tough, he should trust God and keep on going. He now knew how right she had been.

Thanks, Mom.

CHAPTER 55

Behind the counter at the Moon Rock, Sarah was putting on a fresh pot of coffee when she noticed her reflection in the mirror on the wall. She smiled at herself. She was happy and it had to be written all over her face.

She heard the door chime behind her. She glanced up at the mirror and saw it was Mike. She turned to him and smiled, holding up a coffee mug. He nodded and walked over to his usual booth, which was, of course, available.

Sarah walked over to Mike's table and set the mug of steaming coffee on the table. She noticed a thick manila envelope lying on the table. "What do you have there, Mike?"

Mike smiled, then slid the mentoring manual out of the envelope. "What do you think?"

"Mike! I love it! It is so beautiful. I know you must be so happy!" She threw her arms around Mike's neck and hugged him. She let him go and sat down.

"I am happy. I think it turned out great." Mike looked admiringly at the new book.

"It turned out perfect," Sarah agreed. "Your dad would be so proud of you."

Mikes eyes got misty. "Yeah, I think he would be too."

"You are making a difference. Through you, your dad's legacy will live on."

"Thanks, Sarah. That means alot coming from you. I'm just trying to keep up with you. How are things at the Potter's Plate?"

"It's awesome. I love going there and helping out. I guess we're all making a difference in our own way."

Mike nodded, sipping his coffee. "I agree. It's amazing that all of this came about because of the nightmares. My mom used to say that in every bad situation, God could bring about some good. I never really understood that till now."

"I feel the same way."

Mike finished his coffee and stood up. "I hate to run, but I have some things to do. I was thinking of calling Frank and George to ask if they'd like to meet here later. I was thinking around 5 p.m. Is that okay with you?"

"Oh yes. In fact, I'll reach out to Beth and see if she can drop by as well."

Mike slipped the mentoring manual back into the envelope. "Great. I will see you later then." He gave her a quick hug and rushed out the door.

CHAPTER 56

Sarah walked back to the counter and grabbed her cell phone from under the counter. She sent Beth a text telling her about the impromptu meeting and asked her to stop by later if she had the time.

Sarah put her phone back under the counter and got busy serving her customers. She was amazed at herself for enjoying it so much. It was not that long ago that she dreaded going to work. All of the positive changes she had experienced almost made her happy about the nightly dreams. She knew that because of them, and because of Mordecai, her life would never be the same.

She remembered a story her mother used to tell her—that the most beautiful grass always grew in the valley. One might think that the mountaintop was the best place to be, and it is good, but it is the valley where growth really manifests.

The past few weeks had indeed been a valley for Sarah, as well as for Mike and their three new friends, but she would not change it now if she could.

Later on, Sarah's cell chimed as she was serving some new-comers to Moon Rock.

"Hi Sarah, yes count me in. I'll see if Frank can come get

me. I look forward to seeing you guys again. It's only been days and it feels like weeks. Hope all is well. Can't wait to share everything that has happen. All good. Actually amazing. See you soon ;) at 5 p.m."

Sarah was excited about seeing everyone that afternoon. It had only been a few days since they last met, but it felt much longer.

They had all been through so much, and were fortunate to have each other.

CHAPTER 57

Frank drove across the Brooklyn Bridge, on his way to pick up Beth. Unlike his last trip across the bridge, he wasn't holding on to the steering wheel for dear life. He was still nervous, but nothing like before.

He arrived in front of Beth's building right on time.

Beth was waiting on the sidewalk and waved at Frank as he approached. She swung open the back door and hopped in. "Hello, Frank! How are you today?"

"I am doing well, thank you. How are you?"

"I am doing great. Especially after receiving this in the mail." She held up a hot-pink envelope.

"What is that?" he asked.

"It's a thank-you card from my first pro bono client. May I read it to you?"

"Yes, please do." Frank pulled away from the curb.

Beth read the card to Frank, fighting back the tears all over again.

"That's beautiful," he said. "I bet that made your day."

Beth laughed. "Are you kidding me? It made my month!"

Then her levity stopped abruptly. They were on the Brooklyn Bridge.

"Are you okay, Beth?" Frank noticed her sudden change in

mood.

"I'm not sure I will ever get used to being on this bridge, Frank."

"I understand, but it will be fine. I still get a little nervous too, but not as much as before. After everything we have all been through, I feel that everything is going to turn out okay."

Beth and Frank arrived at the Moon Rock without incident. Frank parked in front, then shut off the engine.

"Whew!" Beth said from the back seat. "Thank you, God."

Frank chuckled. "Amen to that!"

They entered the café and found Sarah already waiting at a table. Her shift had ended and she had pastries and coffee waiting in anticipation of her friends' arrival.

Sarah stood and hugged them both, offering them a seat. "It's so good to see you both! How was the drive here?"

"It was fine," Beth and Frank answered in unison. They were all three laughing when the door chimed. It was Mike and George.

Mike sauntered over to the table. "Well, you seem like a happy bunch."

"We *are* a happy bunch!" Beth replied, still laughing.

They all gathered around the table, snacking on pastries and sipping coffee. They each shared recent stories of the opportunities they had for helping others. Sarah told them about her time at the Potter's Plate, and Mike shared about his new mentor program. Frank told them about the free cab rides he had given, and George was helping Habitat for Humanity build a house. Beth retrieved the hot-pink envelope from her briefcase and passed it around the table for all to read.

Suddenly one of Sarah's regulars bolted through the door. "Quick! Turn on the television!" he said, obviously out of breath.

Sarah jumped up from the table. "What's the matter?"

"Just turn on the news. Channel 4. Hurry."

Sarah ran over to the counter, grabbed the remote for the wall-mounted television, and turned it on. She scrolled through the channels and stopped at channel 4.

There was a banner along the bottom of the screen that said *Breaking News*. A young woman was excitedly reporting what had happened. "There has been a multicar pileup on the Brooklyn Bridge. The cause of this horrific accident is not known at this time, but police are investigating. We have a news team en route and we will bring you updates as soon as we have them."

Everyone at the table was silent, staring at the television in awe. Movement near the front window caught Mike's eye. He turned to look and saw Mordecai looking back at him. How long he had been there, Mike did not know. Unable to speak, he elbowed Sarah and pointed toward the window. The others saw his gesture and also looked at the window.

This was not a dream, and yet each one of them saw the man who had visited them in their dreams so many times. He was dressed the same, all black, and had the same calm demeanor. Mordecai looked away from the faces staring at him wide-eyed, and up at the television on the wall. After a moment, he looked back at each person, a lingering smile on his face. Then, he slowly turned and melted into the crowd on the sidewalk.

All five of them sat there, utterly without speech. Tears filled their eyes. They turned once more to see if they could catch one more glimpse of Mordecai. They could see him, off in the distance, weaving his way through the crowd. They shared a chill when they saw his black suit had turned into a pristine white.

Five lives—make that six—forever changed.

*****

"Well done, good and faithful servant!"
—MATTHEW 25:21